TRAIN
—TO—
DESTINY

ERNIE ANDERSON

I0578623

OTHER BOOKS BY ERNIE ANDERSON:

The Release of the Albatross

The Return of the Albatross

Whispers from the Hills

Echoes From the Valley

Copyright © 2021 Ernie Anderson.

All rights reserved. No part of this book may be reproduced,
stored, or transmitted by any means—whether auditory, graphic,
mechanical, or electronic—without written permission of both
publisher and author, except in the case of brief excerpts used
in critical articles and reviews. Unauthorized reproduction of
any part of this work is illegal and is punishable by law.

This book is a work of fiction. Places, events, and situations
in this story are purely fictional. Any resemblance to
actual persons, living or dead is coincidental.

ISBN: 978-1-956373-23-3 (sc)
ISBN: 978-1-956373-24-0 (hc)
ISBN: 978-1-956373-25-7 (e)

Because of the dynamic nature of the Internet, any web addresses or
links contained in this book may have changed since publication and
may no longer be valid. The views expressed in this work are solely those
of the author and do not necessarily reflect the views of the publisher,
and the publisher hereby disclaims any responsibility for them.

I would like to thank all of those who have bought my books and encourage me to continue to write more. A special thank you to Marcia Shipley, my editor, who has been a tremendous help to me in the preparation of this book.

I respectfully dedicate this book to all of the brave men and women who have served our Great Nation in the Armed Forces. To those who gave their lives, to those who fought and now carry the scars and to those who trained and were prepared. I thank you for my freedom, and I heartily salute you. In my eyes, it is you who are America's heroes. May God bless you and God bless America.

CHAPTER

1

It was July 3, 1950 in Greenbrier County, just south of Ronceverte, West Virginia. Mike walked down through the field toward the railroad track. He loved to come there and watch the trains rush by.

The sun was pouring down as if there was a fan behind a heater, blowing the heat down. The past three days of sweltering heat had dried up all the mud puddles from the recent rains, and the grass was starting to wilt and turn brown in places.

Mike walked over and placed a penny on the hot rail. Walking off the track and twenty feet or so up the hill, he turned and sat down and waited. In a few minutes, he looked up and listened intently as he heard the train's whistle off in the distance. It was coming from the west, and he watched as the train came into view. It was approaching quickly and he waved to the engineer, who waved back and gave him a couple of pulls on the whistle.

A sense of excitement and awe overwhelmed Mike as he sat on the bank and watched the train fade into the distance and out of sight. He was fascinated too, by the noise of the engine and the clanging wheels as it hurried to its destination. *I am going to be on one of those trains one day,* he vowed.

Walking to the track, he picked up the now flattened penny, which covered his palm. He slipped it into his jeans hip pocket and went across the track and down the path to the Greenbrier River.

The pristine water flowed over a little natural water fall and continued down to where Mike was standing. It was some thirty feet wide at that point. It was shallow in that area and only about four feet deep at the deepest part in the middle. Little minnows were scurrying along near the shore.

It was scorching hot, and Mike peeled off his clothes and walked out into the shallow water. The water was cold at first, but felt good to him. It was a welcomed relief from the heat of the past three days. In the middle now, he ducked down under the water and washed himself without any soap. He walked back halfway toward the shore and scooped up a hand full of flat pebbles. Throwing them downstream, he watched as they skipped along the top of the water. After tiring of that, he returned to the clothes he had laid on a big rock and got dressed.

Back up the path, and across the tracks, he leisurely strolled. It wasn't time to milk the cows, so he was not in any hurry to return home. He walked up through the field and shortly reached the large frame house where he lived.

He lived on a small farm of fifty acres. They had two cows and usually kept about ten steers. These steers were raised to sell, but sometimes one would be slaughtered when they needed beef to eat. They also had chickens, so Mike had his chores to do around the place.

Even with his chores, he had plenty of time to do the things he liked to do, especially in the summer when he was off from school.

Mike lived with his mother and father, two sisters, and a brother. His father was Henry Clark, who was a coal miner. His mother was Patricia Clark, who was a hard-working housewife. Mike's brother, James, was twenty years old and five years older than Mike. He had worked at the Greenbrier Hotel, in White Sulphur

Springs, since his graduation two years ago from Greenbrier High School in Ronceverte. His two younger sisters were Jessica, who was thirteen, and Candace, who was eleven.

They were not rich, but neither were they poor. They had everything that they needed to maintain a comfortable lifestyle. Perhaps a little more than many people in that area since James was now working and contributing to the household income.

Life was good on the farm. Mike was looking forward to his graduation from Greenbrier High School, known for its first-rate education and its excellent teachers. James had played all the sports in school, and Mike would do the same. The girls were active in the various clubs at school and choirs, etc.

Later that night Mike went up the stairs to his room. He opened the window and immediately felt the cool breeze come through the screen. It had been awfully hot, but cooled off at night and was comfortable enough to sleep with just a sheet for a cover.

Mike placed the flattened penny in a shoebox on his dresser with his other treasures and carefully closed the lid. He then undressed and got into bed. Lying on his back, he waited. In a few minutes he heard the train whistle off in the distance. He slipped out of bed and went over to the window. On his knees, with his arms propped up on the windowsill, he waited and watched. The wailing of the train's whistle was music to his ears and stirred the often-felt excitement within. It was a moonlit night. Mike could see the train quickly approaching, as it raced through the valley, while he looked out across the field. He didn't bother to count the cars filled with coal, since he had counted them so many times in the past. He knew that there were at least a hundred cars, counting the boxcars. He stayed there and watched until the red light on the red caboose faded in the distance.

Returning to bed, he continued his musing. Mike had an adventuresome spirit. *"One day,"* he thought, *"I am going to ride on one of those boxcars and see where it goes. "* It was as if the call of the wild and the unknown was beckoning to him to come aboard.

"Come," he could hear it saying, "Come, and I will show you mighty and wondrous things." He was fascinated with trains; it had been that way for as long as he could remember.

One of Mike's responsibilities was maintaining the family's coal pile. He frequently found chunks of coal along the railroad track, which had fallen off the coal cars, and added these findings to this coal pile. The coal that would occasionally spill off the cars was burned during the winter to heat their house.

Mike's eyes finally became heavy, and he drifted off to sleep.

The next three years for Mike were spent finishing school. He played all the sports, and lettered in all of them, as his older brother had done. He had grown to be quite tall, and had filled out to be a muscular young man. He was handsome with dark brown hair and blue eyes, from his mother's side of the family. Mike had dated a few girls, but no one seriously.

The last four years, since he graduated, he had worked at the hardware store in Ronceverte.

It was now early April in 1957. March had brought with it an abundance of rain that year, and the shrubs and flowers were just beginning to stir from their winter of sleep. Winter was begrudgingly releasing her cold grip on the area. The nights were still quite cold, but it had started to warm up nicely during the day.

With the changing of the season, Mike seemed to become more restless. He had already spoken to his parents about going on a trip. They were concerned for his safety, but understood his restlessness, and had assured him that they wouldn't stand in his way.

Mike had managed to save $2,000 during the past four years of working at the hardware store and part- time at the service station in Ronceverte. He had decided to take $500 with him and leave the rest in his bank account, which his parents could access, should he need it.

Mike had not set a particular date for his departure. He did promise his dad that he would plow the garden for him and get it ready to plant before he left.

Friday, the fourteenth of April, brought the completed garden ready for planting and a decision as to when he would leave. His official goodbyes were said that night. They all wished him well with promises of support, should they be needed in the future. Not one for long goodbyes, Mike went up to his room and packed his new canvas bag, which would serve as his luggage. The bag was about thirty inches in length and eighteen inches high, and a foot wide. It could hold a good amount, and yet was small enough to be easily carried, as well as being very sturdy. After packing and rechecking everything, he turned in for the night. Sleep came quickly, and he rested well in his bed. He would begin his adventure the next day.

Having said his final goodbye to his mother and sisters and, with a good breakfast under his belt, Mike set out walking down the graveled road toward the main road. He tucked the bag of food his mother had prepared for him into his luggage bag and was off.

Reaching the main road, which was Route 219, he did not have to wait long until he hitched a ride with an old farmer who was going to Ronceverte.

"Hop in, Mike; looks like you are going on a trip?"

"Yes sir, Mr. Wilson, I am going west for a while," Mike said, as he put his bag in the bed of the pickup.

"Well, is that so?" Mr. Wilson pulled onto the road as

Mike shut the passenger door.

They soon arrived near Ronceverte, and Mike got out just past the bridge that crosses the Greenbrier River. He thanked him for the ride and retrieved his bag.

He walked two blocks down a little hill, to the railroad tracks, just west of the town. He then walked west along the tracks about a half-mile and went up on the bank to the left of the tracks.

It was nearly eleven o'clock, and the west bound coal and freight train was due in a few minutes. Mike had chosen where he was because the train would be getting up to speed along there, but not so fast that he couldn't hop on it.

He had not mentioned how he would travel, but left the impression that he would hitch hike, or go by bus or train. Not wanting to worry them, he said nothing about hopping a freight train.

Mike stood up and peered around the big oak tree he had been sitting under. He saw the train coming down the track in his direction. The adrenalin started pumping, but he remained where he was, hidden behind the tree.

The engines ambled down the track and soon passed Mike. Mike went down, beside the moving train, and watched the empty coal cars pass him. He saw the boxcars following them in the distance. There were a number of empty boxcars behind the coal cars. Their doors were open, as well as the doors of the caboose.

Mike chose the third boxcar and, when the opened door came up even with him, he threw the canvas bag up and into the boxcar. He then took off running and, grabbing the vertical door-handle, he hoisted himself up and into the doorway of the boxcar. He ended up in the sitting position with his legs dangling out of the doorway. He remained in that position for quite some time as the train rapidly gained speed.

Rolling along through the valleys, he feasted his eyes on the majestic mountains surrounding him. The various flowers and flowering trees were beginning to open up to the warmth of the sun. The unopened buds that remained seemed anxious to burst into bloom and shower the mountains with their brilliant colors. The spectacular scenery seemed to be magnified in the spring, as if each flower was in competition with its companion in a beauty contest. After the dull and gray days of the long winter, spring was not only welcomed for its warmth but, with its arrival, it renewed the beauty, which was given freely for all to enjoy.

The warm spring wind whipped through his hair, and his mind returned to the early days of his youth. He had often wondered how it would feel to do what he was now doing. He remained transfixed, holding the side of the door with one hand. Mike had good feelings about being there and had a sense of accomplishment, even though he had just begun his trip.

With no particular destination in mind, he was content to be fulfilling his dream, and be going just wherever the train went. The times in his youthful past, when he had watched the train from his room, and from beside the tracks, came to mind. Now that he was doing what he had dreamed about, all those times, he seemed to be at peace about it, and felt as if he and the train were partners in this adventure.

The train rolled on; down through the valleys of West Virginia and into Kentucky it sped. The miles of track were quickly crossed, separating Mike further from home.

About four hours into his trip, and well into Kentucky now, Mike dug into his lunch bag and retrieved a country-ham sandwich. He washed it down with the water he had brought along, and then munched on an apple for dessert.

Mike noticed the train slowing down and, standing beside the opened door, he looked out. When the train passed the sign of the town of Mount Sterling, Mike decided he might as well get off here when it slowed enough to jump off safely. The train continued to slow down and was barely moving now.

Mike put his lunch bag in the canvas bag and then threw the canvas bag off the train. He then jumped off the slow-moving train and walked back to pick up his canvas bag. He turned around and walked in the direction of the town.

The train soon passed him and, when the train disappeared, he could see that he was not far from the town. He went over four sets of sidetracks, and over a little hill, as he walked toward the center of town.

Looking toward town, he saw a man leaning against the side of a building just off the tracks. He felt the man's eyes following him as he got nearer to him.

He was about ten years older than Mike, and shabby looking. He watched Mike intently as the distance between them shrunk.

"Hi, Buddy," the stranger said, as Mike approached him carrying the canvas bag. "Hello," Mike said hesitantly.

"I saw you get off that train over there," stated the man.

"I ride the rails myself; waiting now for the west bound freight to Louisville." The man then shoved his hand toward Mike.

"Joe Hill is my name; most people call me Hobo Joe though."

"Mike Clark is my name," Mike said, as he shook his hand. "What time does that train leave for Louisville?" Mike asked, feeling a little more at ease now.

"It will pull out about 9:00P.M."

"You have been riding these rails a while, have you?"

"Yeah, a few years now," he said.

"Well, nice meeting you," said Mike as he started to walk away. "Wait a minute, how about me buying you a cup of coffee? There is a restaurant right over there," he pointed across the street.

"Okay, why not, it's a while before the train comes in."

They walked across the street and into the restaurant.

Slipping the canvas bag underneath the seat, Mike slid into the booth and Joe took the seat across from him.

Joe ordered scrambled eggs, bacon, toast, hash browns and coffee. Mike wasn't hungry yet and ordered coffee. The waitress brought the food, and Joe dug in like he was starving. Mike drank his coffee and watched Joe devour the meal.

"This is good, Mike; don't you want something to eat?"

"No, I am not hungry right now."

Finishing his meal and starting on his coffee refill, Joe pushed the plate aside.

"This is on me, kid," Joe said, reaching into his pocket.

"Uh oh, must have left my wallet in my luggage back at the corner," Joe said. "I'll just slip over there and get it, won't take a minute. I'll be right back."

"Yeah, okay, I'll be here." Mike was wondering about that guy, the way he made haste to get out of there, but he waited and finished his coffee. After having another cup of coffee, Mike went over and paid the bill and left the restaurant. *So, that is the way Mr. Joe Hill is, is it?* Mike thought.

Mike walked down the street of the small town and soon crossed over and headed back toward the track. Arriving back at the corner where he had met Joe, Mike looked all around, but he was nowhere in sight.

Mike went around the corner of the building and looked across the tracks in the rail yard. He sat down and leaned against the building, waiting for the train to come along. Mike sat there for a while and then got up and started walking to the west, out of the town. On the outskirts of town there was only one set of tracks. Mike went well down the tracks before going up a little bank where he sat and waited for the train.

Looking back toward the town, he saw the engines backing up on the sidetracks and picking up cars. Then in a little while, here it came down the track toward Mike.

As Mike watched the train coming closer, he began looking for a boxcar with open doors. He spotted one and, when the engines had passed, he got down near the track and kept his eyes on the opened boxcar. As the opened door came up even with him, he heaved his bag aboard and then ran, grabbing onto the handle to hoist himself up and into the car. The train was picking up speed rapidly. *"Next time,"* Mike thought, *"I'll get a little closer to the town."*

Looking around inside the boxcar, Mike saw that he was not alone. There was straw on each end of the box car, and sitting in the east end corner was a guy with a moustache, wearing coveralls. Mike spoke to him, and the guy nodded and sort of grunted. Having dealt enough with strangers today, Mike moved to the other end of the car and, placing his bag beside him, got out his snack bag.

He started eating another ham sandwich and noticed that the guy was watching his every move. Feeling a little guilty, he reached into his bag and retrieved another sandwich and held it up as if asking a question. The guy held his two palms up. Mike tossed the sandwich to him and, when he caught it, he began to eat vigorously. *"Everybody I meet is hungry,"* thought Mike.

Mike noticed how small the guy's hands were and how smooth his face was. The guy's baseball cap was pulled low down over his forehead.

Mike took an apple out and held it up for the guy to see. He opened his palms again, and Mike tossed it to him.

The guy quickly finished the sandwich and began eating the apple. Mike then took one of the bottles of water from his bag and held it up. The guy held his palms out and caught the bottle when he threw it to him.

"Thank you" the guy said, in a strange, sort of deep voice.

"You are more than welcome," replied Mike.

Mike got up and walked over to the opened door, holding onto the side of the car for support. The train was running at full speed now, and the wind whipped his hair as he stood and looked out into the night. The full moon flickered as if someone was rapidly turning the pages of a book while they sped by the trees along the track. Then, for a time, the trees disappeared when they arrived at an open area. An open field was revealed before him with horses off in the distance. An overwhelming feeling of excitement filled Mike as he remembered watching the trains pass by him in the days of his youth. He was thrilled to be fulfilling his dreams of long ago and have a part in the train's journey. An occasional mournful wail from the train's whistle, when it passed a crossing, only intensified these feelings.

Glancing over at his unnamed companion, he saw that he had fallen asleep, lying there in the straw. Looking closer, he noticed that the black moustache had slipped down on one side across his companion's lip. *"What is with this guy?"* He thought. *"Why the phony moustache?"* Turning back to the opened door, Mike continued his enjoyment of the warm spring wind blowing on his face and tossing his hair about. A long gradual right-turn, around the mountain, now revealed the sight of the four engines as they pulled the train forward.

He remained there for a few minutes, and then got up and made his way to the end of the boxcar. He raked the straw up into the corner with his foot and made a comfortable bed. It had been a long and busy day, and he settled down in the straw, feeling the need to rest. He was there only a short time when his eyes became heavy and the rocking of the car, along with the melodious clicking of the steel wheels, drew him into a deep sleep.

The next morning, Mike suddenly opened his eyes when the train jerked and bumped as it coupled with another railroad car. The bright sunlight cascaded through the opened doors on each side of the car. He stretched and leaned up against the back of the car and noticed his companion was standing in the doorway.

"Where are we?" Mike asked, waking up now.

"St Louis, Missouri." He answered in a high voice. Mike got up and walked over to the door where his companion stood. When he turned to look at him, he noticed that the moustache was no longer there.

"You must have shaved while I was asleep," he said. His companion then looked over at him, grinning, and removed the hat. When the hat came off, beautiful brown hair fell down around a creamy complexion.

"I thought I'd have a better chance as a guy, but when I woke up with the moustache in my mouth, I thought a caterpillar had crawled into my mouth." They both laughed. When she laughed, Mike noticed she had perfect teeth, which were absolutely pearly white. The tension between them dissipated immediately.

"Want to get some breakfast? I don't know about you, but I am hungry," asked Mike.

"Yes, I am hungry too, we'd better get off before the switchman sees us," she said.

The train was moving slowly as they threw their bags off and then eased themselves down off the boxcar.

Retrieving their bags, they walked across the numerous tracks toward the city.

Looking down the tracks, they saw a switchman working, attaching the air hoses between newly coupled cars. They increased their pace and soon arrived on the sidewalk just off of the tracks.

It was not a good part of town. Several of the businesses along there had long since closed up shop, and the residents had moved on. They passed a run-down bar that looked as if it never closed. There was a shabbily dressed old man, lying in a doorway of a boarded up business a couple of doors down, apparently sleeping it off as he cradled in his arm an empty whiskey bottle.

Mike and his companion picked up the pace and hurried to get through the slums, which they had chosen as their disembarkation point.

"Spare me a dollar?" asked one of the two guys standing in a doorway as they went by. Mike said nothing, but reached over and grabbed his companion's arm protectively, and hurried past them.

They arrived at an intersection and crossed the street.

After the two-block hike from the tracks, things began to look better. They found a decent looking diner and entered. Taking an isolated booth, Mike slid into the booth and looked at the girl before she sat down.

"Why don't you go on to the bathroom, and then you can watch the bags when I go?"

"Okay, I'll be right back," she said. She moved off to the bathroom, and Mike picked up the menu. The girl came back just as the waitress was coming over with water and utensils.

"Order number three for me, if you will, and I'll be right back," he told her, moving off to the bathroom.

He returned shortly to find waiting for him a plate of bacon and eggs with hash browns, and a steaming cup of coffee.

"My name is Mike Clark from Ronceverte, West Virginia," he said, extending his hand across the booth.

"I am Rebecca Jefferies, and I am from Beckley, West Virginia," she said, taking his hand.

"My friends call me Reba," she smiled.

Mike noticed the softness of her hand. He began to devour his breakfast, as did Reba.

They continued to talk as they ate their breakfast. Mike told her his story, and she shared with him her own story and why she was there. Her father had died in the coalmines five years ago, and her mother had married another man a year after that. He was verbally abusive to her and tried to run her life. She had become fed up with it and decided to leave there and pursue her dream of going to Hollywood. After winning a couple of beauty contests, and saving a few hundred dollars, she decided to strike out on her own. She had tried to look like a man, thinking she would have a better chance out in the world, and that was the reason for the moustache.

Reba was very popular in high school. She was also athletic and had an adventuresome spirit. It didn't seem to faze her to be out in the world, on her own, crossing the country, to pursue her dream of becoming a Hollywood star. She didn't like being around her controlling step father, so that was a big factor in her decision to strike out on her own. There weren't many things Reba was afraid of; however; with her step-father's constant verbal abuse and controlling demeanor, she was becoming fearful of her own retaliations, should she remain at home. She had, therefore, chosen to separate herself from the situation at home.

Mike couldn't help but notice her beauty as he sat talking to her. She had dark brown hair and translucent green eyes. Her face was creamy and smooth. He could see her becoming a movie star with those looks.

Finishing their breakfast, Mike reached for the check, when she intercepted him.

"I'll get this," she said, "you bought my supper, remember?"

"Aw, that was nothing," he said.

"Yes, it was, I was really hungry and it was delicious," she said, walking to the counter with the check in hand.

Mike left a tip, and they exited the restaurant onto the street.

Not wanting to retrace their steps through the ghetto part of the city, they decided to turn west and walk a couple of blocks to see if the area was any better. After going about four blocks, it looked better, and they headed for the tracks.

Arriving there, they headed west along the tracks. It was a long walk to get out of the city. The warmth of the spring sun felt good on their faces as they trudged on down the tracks. After walking about two miles, they sat down under an overpass along the tracks.

In about thirty minutes, a passenger train came by, slowly gaining speed as it went by them. They waited about another hour and then watched the approaching freight train as the four engines passed them. The engineer waved at them as he passed by. They waved back as if to thank him for the ride he was about to give them.

Readying themselves along the track until a promising boxcar came along beside them; they heaved their bags aboard and then ran and hoisted themselves up and onto the boxcar. Looking around, they found that they had made a good choice. The car was reasonably clean with a little straw in each end, along with some cardboard that had been left there.

"What's wrong?" Mike said, as he looked at Reba, holding her side.

"I don't know, I got a sharp pain when I pulled up," she said.

"It is easing up now, maybe I just strained my side," she added. She straightened up and apparently the pain had subsided.

Mike set about to stow their bags in one end of the car.

"Maybe you better lie down a while," he said, as the train gained speed.

"Yes, maybe I will," she said, and went over to the bags and sat down, leaning up against her duffle bag.

Mike went over and sat at the door and looked at the flat fields pass by as they sped down the track. Glancing over at Reba, he hoped she would be all right.

"She sure is pretty," he thought, not letting her see him looking at her.

CHAPTER

3

Reba soon went to sleep, and Mike stayed at the door as the train proceeded hurriedly toward its destination. Occasionally, he would glance over at Reba. After a couple of hours of sleep, she awoke and sat up and stretched.

"Hi, Mike, where are we?" she asked, coming over to where he was at the door.

"We'll be coming into Kansas City in a few minutes."

"Wonder if this train goes through, or if we should get off?" she asked.

"I guess we'll wait and see what the train does," he said.

The whistle wailed, and the train began to slow down. Mike looked around the side of the opened door and saw that they were approaching the city. The busy train yard was just ahead and Mike stood up, keeping a watchful eye along the track ahead.

The train slowed more and was barely moving now.

"I think they are going to drop some cars, maybe we had better get off," he said.

Mike noticed a yardman heading back toward them, some five cars back. The train soon stopped, and he went across to the other side of the car and looked out.

16

No one was in sight, and he looked out and saw the city off to that side.

"Quick, get the bags. We need to get off before that guy gets up this far," he urged.

Reba got Mike's bag as he looked out of the train. He threw it off and slipped off the train. Turning around, he took her bag and laid it on the ground beside his. Then he reached up and helped her get off the train. Hurriedly, they grabbed their bags and scurried across the several tracks toward the city.

Going up a little hill from the tracks, they spotted a service station and went in to the bathroom. Mike finished first and waited outside, drinking a coke, until Reba came out. She got a coke and they headed up the street.

Mike didn't notice for a minute that Reba had fallen behind and, when he turned to see where she was, he noticed her bent over in pain some ten feet behind him.

"What is the matter?' he said, going back to her.

"It's that pain again, and its worse this time," she said. "We better get you to a doctor," he said, noticing that she had begun to sweat profusely. He helped her sit down along the sidewalk.

"I am going for help. You wait here," he said, putting his bag behind her to lean on. Mike ran back to the service station and asked the girl behind the counter to call for help. He then went back to Reba and waited. In just a few minutes an ambulance pulled up beside them, and they put Reba on a stretcher and into the back. Mike crawled into the ambulance and sat beside her. They soon reached the hospital, and Reba was rushed into the emergency room. Mike waited in the emergency room waiting room. In a few minutes a nurse came out and told Mike that Reba had a bad appendix and would need surgery immediately. Mike asked if he could see her. The nurse said he could see her briefly, and led him back to the examining room.

Looking at her, he saw that she was sweating and looked confused.

"Reba, can I call someone or do anything to help you?" he asked.

"No, no use to call anybody now. I'll call them later," she said.

"I am sorry to be a drag on you, Mike; you can go on, if you want to."

"No, I'll be right here with you when you wake up. Don't worry, I'll help you however I can.

"Thanks, Mike," she said, through a painful smile.

"I will have to take her back now. I'll come and get you when it is over," the nurse said.

Mike returned to the waiting room and took a seat on a big comfortable chair.

"I hope she does well with the surgery," he thought, *"Lucky we got off the train when we did."*

Mike laid his head back and dozed for a while.

The next thing he knew, the nurse was calling his name and shaking his shoulder.

"Reba did fine. She is in her room now. You can go up and see her, if you want to. She is in Room 304,"she said. "Thanks, I'll go right up there," he said, getting up and heading for the elevator.

Mike went in to see her and found her alone. He walked over beside the bed and, noticing the clock, he realized it had been three hours since they arrived at the hospital.

"Are you asleep?" he asked in a low voice, looking down at her in the bed.

"No, not really," she said, opening her eyes lazily. "Here is your bag," he said, setting it down on a chair by the window.

Mike sat in a chair beside the bed with his arm resting on the bed. She turned and looked at Mike.

"Mike, I appreciate all you've done for me," she said.

"No problem; I am just glad that you came through it all right, and glad we got here in time."

"Did they say how long you would be in here?" he asked.

"They said two or three days, if I did well," she said.

"Why don't you go ahead on your way and maybe I'll catch up with you sometime?" she said.

"No, I'm not on any schedule; I'll wait for you to get better. That is, if you want me to."

"Thanks Mike," she said, taking her hand out from under the cover and squeezing his hand, not turning it loose.

Mike felt a little warm, and didn't know exactly what to think, but he liked the feel of her soft hand in his.

"Well, I am glad you got the surgery over with and are now on the mend," he said, looking at her.

"I guess I had better go and find a place to stay tonight," he said.

She hadn't taken her eyes off of Mike and continued looking at him as he stood up. When he stood up, she pulled his hand down to her and kissed the back of it.

"Thanks, Mike. Be careful, and call me tomorrow, okay?"

"Yes, I will, and I'll be back tomorrow to see you. Just rest. I hope you feel better."

"Okay, goodnight Mike," she said, as he moved off to the door.

Carrying his bag, Mike went to the elevator and found his way out of the hospital.

Out on the street, he looked both ways and decided to go right and to the center of town. He soon saw a hotel sign up ahead and made his way toward it. Arriving there, he saw that it wasn't a very classy place, but not a dump either, so he went in and took a room on the second floor. At least it was close to the hospital, and he was glad to put the bag down and relax a while.

Mike took a long shower and went to bed. It felt good to be in a regular bed again. Sleep came quickly.

He awoke to the sound of a vacuum cleaner running in the hallway. Looking at his watch, he saw that it was 9:00 A.M. He got up and went to the bathroom and then got dressed. He stopped in the lobby, where they had free coffee, and he got a cup and walked outside.

He sat down on a bench in front of the hotel and drank his coffee. The sun was shining brightly, and he noticed across the street that they were just coming out of the ground with a new building. He walked over to the construction office trailer and inquired about a temporary job. They said they could use him, and he told them that he could start that afternoon at 1:00 P.M. With that settled, he went down the street to a restaurant and had a big breakfast.

After breakfast, Mike walked down the street and found a department store on the way to the hospital. He went in and bought Reba a long sleeve plaid shirt and a pair of new jeans. Putting them under his arm, he went on down to the hospital to see Reba. She was standing, looking out the window, when he entered her room.

"Good morning," he said, as he walked over to her.

"Hi, Mike," she said, returning to the bed.

"You must be doing all right, getting up already?"

"Yes, I am doing good, just a little weak."

"That's good. I brought you something," he said, handing the bag to her.

"Mike, you shouldn't have done that. What is it?" she said, opening the bag.

"Oh, thanks, Mike, I wonder if they fit?" she said, holding the jeans up. "I'll try them on later."

"If they don't fit, you can exchange them; the store is just up the street."

"By the way, I got a job, and I rented a room for a week," he said.

"I thought maybe you would be better and ready to travel by then."

"Maybe so. The doctor said I was doing fine and could stay one or two more nights and then be released."

"That is great," said Mike, "you can continue to recuperate in the hotel room, and I'll work during the day."

"What would I have done without you, Mike?" she said, looking up at him.

"Well, it isn't like I am on any schedule or anything, just playing it as it comes."

"Well, I had better go get ready to go to work; I am supposed to go in at one o'clock this afternoon."

"Okay, Mike, and thanks for everything, I love the clothes," she said, standing up and looking at him.

Mike went back to the job site and went to work. They had him helping the bricklayers, keeping them supplied with bricks and mortar. It was hard work, and he was glad when the whistle sounded and they were finished for the day at 4:30P.M.

Mike was starving, so he went right to the restaurant and ate before going to the hotel. After eating, he went to his room and enjoyed a long shower. The water felt good and relaxed his sore muscles. He then got out some fresh clothes, dressed, and went to the hospital. It was about seven o'clock when he got to the hospital.

When he arrived at her room, he knocked on the closed door, and the nurse opened it.

"You can come in, I am just finishing up here," she said, moving a little cart out of the door.

Mike went in, and the door closed behind him. Reba was standing there, dressed in her new clothes.

"What do you think?" she said, smiling and turning around showing off her clothes.

"I think you look great," he said.

The clothes fit her perfectly and he saw, for the first time, the curves she had been hiding behind the coveralls.

"Wow," he thought, *"what a knockout. She is really a beauty."* She had showered and had her hair pulled back behind her ears, and she looked gorgeous with those sparkling eyes.

She noticed his pink complexion, and came over to him and reached up and kissed him on the cheek.

"Thanks, Mike, for the clothes; it was really sweet of you."

As she reached up, Mike's hands went to her waist, and he felt her against him when she reached up. She stayed there just a minute and then turned and went back to the bed and sat on the side of it.

"So, how did the work go this afternoon?" she said, giving Mike some relief by changing the subject. "Oh, it went fine," he said, coming back to earth.

They continued to chat for what seemed like a long time. Getting to know each other, they found plenty to talk about. Mike seemed to relax now and opened up to her more as they talked. Before they knew it, it was time for him to go.

She walked to the door with him and, when he put his hand on the door handle, she put her hand on his. He turned, and their eyes met and locked on each other. By the way they looked at each other; each one seemed to confirm the other's feelings. His hands found her waist again, and her hand moved up his arm to around his neck, along with the other one, as he pulled her into him. Each one's lips found the other's as they hungrily embraced, and a flood of held-back passion was released. Staying there for a while, they finally came up for air and held each other tightly, as if they were holding a helium balloon and, if one let go, it would release the other to fly away. After another passionate embrace, they released each other.

"You feel good," said Mike, looking at her.

"I have to go, but I sure don't want to," he said.

"I don't want you to go either, but I know you must," she said, as she looked up, pulling him down into another passionate embrace.

They kissed and held each other tightly for another minute, and then he said goodnight and left the room.

Reba returned to the bed, got undressed, and lay down with a smile on her face. *He sure did feel good, so good, "* she thought. *"I can hardly wait until tomorrow."*

She was like a little kid who wanted to hurry up and go to sleep so Santa Claus could come. She soon drifted off into a peaceful sleep.

Mike arrived back at the hotel and, going up the elevator to his room, he was still reliving the passion he had just felt with Reba. *"Man, what a beauty, and she felt great in my arms, "* he thought.

He went into his room and got undressed. Slipping into bed, he was still thinking about her. He set the alarm clock and then turned the light off and rolled over. He drifted into a dreamless sleep in five minutes.

Mike had a spring in his step and a smile on his face as he walked to work the next morning. It was only a short distance from the restaurant where he had breakfast, and he was anxious to start the day's work so that it would end and he could once again go see Reba. He had not ceased to think about her since he left her the night before. He called her during the lunch hour, and she was as enthusiastic about him as he was about his visiting her last night.

The day went by fast, and Mike was not nearly as sore as he thought he would be from the hard work. The whistle sounded, and Mike hurried down the street toward the hotel. There was a barbershop in the lobby of the hotel, and he went in and got a haircut before going up to his room.

He felt good about working. Earning some money kept him from dipping into his money that he had brought with him.

He showered and shaved and was anxious to go see

Reba. After putting on his new jeans and his nicest shirt, he went out and headed for the elevator.

He soon arrived at the hospital and went up to Reba's room. When he got there, the door was open and a housekeeper was clearing away her tray and straightening up the room.

"I'll be finished in just a few minutes, sir," she said, as she noticed Mike start to enter the room.

"Yes Ma'am, that is fine. I'll just wait out here," he said, noticing Reba smiling as she waved to him.

Mike waited a few minutes until the lady finished her work.

"There you are; you can go in now, sir," she said, as she moved past Mike and went down the hall.

Mike entered the room and closed the door.

"Hi, Mike," Reba said, as she walked toward him with opened arms. Mike didn't have time to return the greeting, since they began right where they had left off the night before. If anything, it was even more passionate and urgent than before. Becoming better acquainted now, their dreams of the past several hours quickly became reality as they passionately embraced and hungrily exchanged kisses.

"What has come over us, Mike?" she managed to get out.

"I don't know, but if I am dreaming, please don't wake me now," he replied.

They finally walked together to the bed and sat down beside each other and looked out the window.

"I can leave tomorrow, the doctor said."

"That's great, did he say what time?"

"He said I could leave after lunch, about one o'clock.

"I will come and get you and walk with you to the hotel," Mike said as he looked into her eyes. "One thing about it, everything is convenient here," he continued.

"Mike, are you sure? I mean, do you want me to stay there with you?" she said apprehensively. "I never, I haven't ever, I mean, oh, I don't know what I mean."

"All I know is that I have not ceased to think about you since the other night when you held me like you did," she said, looking down at her hands clasped together in her lap.

"Don't worry, there is no obligation; but, you do need a place to recuperate," Mike said, placing his hand on hers.

"I will be working during the day and you can rest and get better."

"I think about you too, all the time," he said.

She leaned her head over on his shoulder and then looked up and her eyes found his. Sliding his arm around her, he drew her close and they embraced. Their lips hungrily met, seeking to find the taste of sweetness they found in a prolonged exchange of passion.

"Oh, Mike, I have never felt so excited and wantonly about anyone," she confessed.

"I feel the same way. I think you are wonderful, and I am glad we met on the train," he said.

"Yes, oh yes, I am glad too. What would I have done without you? And now I am falling for you, and I can't help myself," she said, tightening her arms around him. They remained there for some time until visiting hours were over, and Mike had to leave and return to the hotel. They talked softly about their plans to go further west when she was able to travel.

He reluctantly left her and walked back to his room, filled with excitement and the thoughts of his new girl friend. Arriving there, he undressed and went to bed. In a few minutes, he heard the wail of a train's whistle, as the train passed through the city, and rolled over with a smile on his face as sleep overtook him.

Morning came quickly and greeted Mike with the cascading of the sunlight streaming through the window. *It's going to be another beautiful day,* he thought, as he headed for the bathroom.

His thoughts turned to Reba as he walked across the street to the restaurant for breakfast. After eating, he went to work, anxious for the time to pass so that he could go get her.

The work had been good for him. His muscles were getting harder, and it helped to keep him in good physical condition. He still did his exercises every day as he had done since he was a boy, wrestling on the team. Mike was a handsome young man and very strong. He had never been one to back down from anyone. He didn't like bullies and, usually, if he was in a fight, he was standing up for someone against one. They soon learned that they could not bully him and get away with it.

Lunchtime arrived quickly as Mike was very busy hauling bricks and mortar to the bricklayers. They had asked him to work on Saturday, and he told them he would. He got an hour off after lunchtime so he could take Reba to the hotel. Mike got a quick bite to eat at the restaurant and then went directly over to the hospital.

When he got there, Reba was already packed and was waiting for the doctor to come by to release her.

When Mike went into her room, she greeted him with a big bear hug and kiss.

"I've been thinking about you all morning," she said, as they walked to the bed and sat down on it.

"I couldn't wait to see you. How do you feel?" Mike said.

"I feel good, just a little weak yet, and the doctor said to take it easy for a while," she answered.

Just then the doctor came in and talked a few minutes before releasing her from the hospital. Gathering up her bag and all of her belongings, they left the hospital and walked down the street to the hotel.

Arriving in the room, Mike put the things down and went over and hugged Reba, and then turned the bed down for her.

"You had better rest now," he said.

Reba went into the bathroom and returned, wearing a cotton nightgown. "Yes, I think I will rest a while," she said, walking over and leaning up against Mike.

"Thanks, Mike, for all you've done for me," she said, looking up at him.

"No problem," he said

After sharing a kiss, she got into bed, and Mike went back to work.

Finishing his day's work, Mike went right to the hotel room and found Reba sound asleep. He went into the bathroom and showered and shaved and, when he came out, Reba looked up and smiled at him.

Mike was standing there in his shorts when she held her arms toward him.

"Come here Mike, I missed you," she said.

Mike went over and lay down beside her. They embraced on the bed, releasing only a portion of their pent-up emotions.

"Oh, Mike, I want you so much, but the doctor said I have to take it easy for a while."

"Yes, you have to get all healed up, and I am not going anywhere. I want you, too. I can't help but want you."

They kissed lovingly and held each other. "Say, are you hungry?" Mike asked.

"Yes, I am hungry. Let me go to the bathroom and get cleaned up, and we'll go eat. I know you must be hungry, after working so hard." she said.

Reba got ready, and they went to a restaurant a couple of blocks up the street. After a good meal, they leisurely walked across the street to a little park and sat on a bench. An old man was busy across the way throwing seed for the pigeons that surrounded him. The night was pleasantly warm, and just a hint of a breeze blew Reba's hair away from her face.

"It sure is nice out tonight," Reba said, looking over at Mike.

"Yes, it is especially nice since you are here and out of the hospital," he said.

"I'll be fine in a few days," she said.

They sat there a while and then walked back to their hotel room. They talked a long time in the room and, later on, when they were both sleepy, they decided to go to bed. Mike embraced her gently. Eventually, they fell asleep in each other's arms.

The next three days seemed to fly by, and it was Saturday before they knew it. Reba had made great progress in her recovery and walked over to have lunch with Mike each day. The hotel room had been paid through Saturday night. That night, in their room, they were talking.

"I think I can travel now, Mike, if you want to head west tomorrow," Reba said.

"Are you sure you are healed enough to travel?"

"Yes, I am healed enough for anything," she said grinning at him. Mike walked over to the bed where she was leaning up against the pillow.

"Oh, are you sure?" he said. "I mean I wouldn't want you to have a relapse or anything. We could wait another week, and I could work until you have more time to heal." He sat down beside her.

"Well, perhaps that would be better; if you are sure you don't mind."

"No, I don't mind at all. I'll pay the room for another week, and just report back to work on Monday. They need the help and will be glad I am staying another week."

They went to bed, and all of their fantasies of the previous days became realities, gently and thoroughly, throughout the night. Pent-up emotions were released as each one of them freely and enthusiastically shared the other's passion with eager abandonment. Reba convinced Mike that she was healed enough for some things, anyway. Some time in the early hours of the morning they drifted into a peaceful sleep, with her head resting on his chest.

The next morning they continued what they had started the night before and then dozed a while. The day was spent getting to know each other better. They did some sightseeing around the city and, later on in the afternoon, they went to a different restaurant for a great meal.

The following week flew by as Mike worked and Reba rested and healed from her surgery. She got stronger very quickly, and her young body was soon well on the way to full recovery.

Mike once again said his goodbyes to the guys on the job that Saturday and headed to the hotel.

Entering the room he found Reba packing her bag. "Looks like you are going on a trip," he smiled at her.

"Yes, I am going across country to California with my special man," she said, running to him with opened arms. They embraced as if they hadn't seen each other for a long time. Mike cleaned himself up and they went to dinner and then back to the hotel.

"How are you Reba, do you feel like traveling now?" he asked.

"Oh yes, I am fine now, and the extra week did help quite a bit," she said. They talked a while and then went to bed.

Suddenly a train's whistle wailed, and they looked at each other and smiled.

"Our ride is calling us," Mike said.

"I hope that doesn't mean that the honeymoon is over," she said.

"No, it is just beginning," he said, as he pulled her closer to him. The honeymoon continued throughout the night. They finally drifted off to sleep in the wee hours.

The next morning Mike awoke and glanced at the clock.

"We had better get moving; it is 9:00A.M." he said. They scurried out of bed and, after showering, they got dressed. Packing up their belongings, they checked out of the hotel and headed for the railroad tracks. They walked a couple of miles to the outskirts of the city and waited for a train to come by. They didn't have to wait long until a freight train came along. They watched as the long row of coal cars passed them by, and then came the freight cars. Choosing their car, they threw their bags up and then ran and hoisted themselves up into the car.

They pulled their bags to one end of the car. Sitting down and, while leaning against their bags, they began to inspect their surroundings. The boxcar appeared clean with only a roll of stiff wire in the comer of their end and just some straw in the other end. They decided that it had been a good choice.

Just then, two bags were thrown into the car from the opposite side from where they had entered. National Bank of Kansas City was written on the side of the bags. Two men then made their way up and into the car.

"Well, what do have we here?" one of them said.

They each sat down at the other end of the car, pulling the bags over to where they were. Both men were shabbily dressed. One appeared to be Oriental, or Mexican, and the other an American. They hurriedly emptied the bank bags of the money they contained and stuffed the bills into a satchel that the taller one had opened. They threw the emptied bags toward the doorway, but the wind blew them to Mike's side just below his feet.

Reba fearfully looked at Mike, and he placed his arm protectively around her. The two men looked capable of anything, and Mike tightened his hold on Reba.

"Jack, what are we going to do with them?" the short Oriental-looking one said.

"I need to get some sleep, Lewis, you take first watch and we'll decide that later," the tall one said.

"Yeah, okay. Go ahead; I'll wake you in a couple of hours," he answered.

The tall one stretched out on the straw and was sleeping in a few minutes.

"You two just stay put and don't give me any trouble," said the little guy.

Then the little man pulled out a pistol and pointed it at them.

"You try anything, and I'll plug you," he said.

Neither Mike nor Reba said anything. Reba had closed her eyes and continued to lean up against Mike. Mike looked out the door of the train moving at full speed now.

"I have to get us off this train, " he thought.

The tall man was snoring loudly now, and the rocking of the train was causing the eyes of the other man to become heavy. He still had the pistol pointing toward Mike, but his eyes were becoming heavier as they moved along. Mike silently watched the hand holding the gun as it rested on the man's leg. Then the man drifted off to sleep and the weight of the gun pulled it out of his hand and it fell silently into the straw beside the man's leg.

Mike reached over and turned Reba's face toward him with his hand. At the same time, he removed his arm from around her and placed his index finger over his lips as Reba opened her eyes and looked at him. She understood and nodded affirmatively to him.

Mike silently reached over and got the small roll of stiff wire and began to straighten it out. When he had unrolled some ten feet of it, he bent a hook on the end of the wire and slowly and carefully pushed the wire toward the gun. When the hook had proceeded to within three inches of the gun, Mike lifted the stiff wire and pushed it forward over the trigger guard and lowered it, hooking the trigger guard with the hook. He then slowly pulled the gun toward him until it was at his feet. Then he hooked the two moneybags, from the National Bank of Kansas City, in like-fashion, pulling them to him. He gave the bags to Reba. He once again hooked the trigger guard and lowered the gun into one of the bags that Reba now held open. Laying the wire aside, Mike put the bagged gun into the other bag. Using the attached string on the bag, he tied the bags closed.

Mike once again turned to Reba and placed his index finger over his lips, silently speaking to himself as much as he was speaking to her. She nodded in response, and Mike stood up and moved slowly toward the opened door. He set the bags beside the door and motioned for Reba to hand him the bags of their belongings. Moving them beside the bank bags, he motioned for Reba to join him by the door.The train continued to speed down the tracks as Mike and Reba waited for an opportunity to exit. They waited for some fifteen minutes, poised to jump off the train at the most opportune moment. When they passed a sign for Salina, the train began to slow down. Mike looked over at the two sleeping beauties and turned back to Reba. The train continued to slow as the robbers slept on.

Looking up ahead, Mike saw a built-up area coming where some tall grass was growing on a slight incline from the tracks. He pointed it out to Reba, indicating that it would be their point of departure. The train slowed more, and Mike grabbed his bag and got ready to toss it off. He motioned for Reba to toss her bag when he tossed his, as the predetermined exit spot drew nearer. They arrived there and tossed their bags off the boxcar. Mike then signaled with his nodding head for Reba to jump, which she did. Mike immediately grabbed the bags containing the gun and jumped out the door. They landed on the tall grass, which cushioned their fall, and rolled to the bottom of the incline. Mike rushed over to Reba.

"Are you all right?" he asked expectantly.

"Yes, I am fine, how about you?" she replied.

"Yes, no problem," he said, as he moved off to collect their bags. Reba got up, brushing her clothing, and watched the train as it continued down the track.

There was a road some 100 yards off the track, which is where they headed. They soon flagged down a car, and headed off to the nearest service station and a phone. They called the police, who soon arrived, and they told them their story of what had happened and turned over the gun to them.

"Yes, we heard of the bank robbery and we'll get on this right away," said the policeman. He then called the police chief and told them to watch the fourth car from the a certain point. The caboose, and to call the railroad people and have them stop the train when it reached plan to capture them had thus been activated.

"I would like you to come to the station and make a statement, if you would," he said to Mike. "Yes, we can do that," he said.

"Good, you can ride with me." he said, pointing to his car.

"I think there is a reward for those guys' capture, but

I haven't heard how much it is," said the officer, on the way to the police station.

"If we get them, you would be eligible for it," he added.

"Apparently a bank teller was shot during the robbery and is in the hospital at last report." said the officer.

They arrived at the police station and wrote out their statement. After leaving their names and addresses, they were free to go and walked out of the police station.

With enough excitement for one day, they decided to look for a room for the night. They soon found a decent hotel, a couple of blocks away, and checked in. They took their bags to the room and then went out and had a good meal.

Back in the room later, Mike turned to Reba.

"You didn't pull anything loose, did you?" he asked. "No, I didn't get hurt, thanks to that tall grass. That made it easy," she said.

They showered and went to bed, feeling fortunate to have gotten out of a difficult situation unscathed. They proceeded to celebrate their victory of getting away from the thugs.

The next morning they called the police station, learning that the robbers had somehow slipped away and the police had not succeeded in their attempt to capture them. The police also said the fingerprints found on the gun matched the robbers' prints, and they would now be charged with murder, since the bank teller had died in surgery. The robbers had been identified as Jack Huffner and Lewis Cruz, ex-convicts, who were on parole. These two were suspected in other robberies in that area recently, and would be put away for a long time, maybe for life, if and when they were caught. The police chief told Mike that they would contact them through his address if he needed to reach him. He also told them that they would be considered for the reward of twenty thousand dollars when they caught the robbers.

"Reba, we were lucky to get away from those guys! I hope they catch them soon," Mike said as he hung up the phone.

"Oh my goodness, I know we were lucky, and I am so glad you were there with me," she said.

Mike called his mother and told her everything that had happened and assured her that they were all right. He wanted her to know what had happened in case the police sent mail there or called on the phone.

They then showered and got dressed and checked out of the hotel. After a big breakfast, they went to the tracks and headed west along the tracks. They didn't have to wait very long until a freight came along. They hopped on, and were on their way. On through Kansas and into Colorado, they went.

Arnvmg in Denver that night, they disembarked and soon found a hotel in which to spend the night. After checking into the hotel, they went out for a good meal.

Mike and Reba were becoming very close in such a short time. Their relationship had progressed, not only physically, but they were becoming more in tune with each other in many ways. Mike was crazy about Reba, and her feelings for him were reciprocated.

After their meal, they returned to the hotel, had long showers, and then went to bed.

The night quickly passed, and they were up and out of there for a good breakfast and then to the tracks.

Mike and Reba were soon heading west, through the magnificent Rocky Mountains. As they sat side by side in the doorway of the boxcar, they were awestruck and almost speechless while watching the mountains appear as the train sped down the track.

"Mike, isn't it just beautiful? Look at those mountains with the snow on top. It is just perfect, being here with you and seeing these mountains for the first time. They are so big, and stand so majestic and proud."

"Yes, it is fantastic being here with you and going on this journey. And it is exciting, just as I envisioned it when I was small. Of course, I didn't know that you would be in the picture at that time, and that makes it that much better."

"We do have a good time together, don't we?" she mused, grinning at Mike.

"Indeed we do, and there is more to come."

On through the beautiful valleys and canyons they sped, through Colorado and into Utah. The train was moving at a fast clip, and they were jostled about occasionally as the train hit a rough place on the track.

Later that night Mike and Reba, becoming tired after a long day, made their way to one end of the boxcar as the train moved hurriedly down the track. They stacked some cardboard up in one corner and, using their bags as pillows, they decided to sleep for a while. They both soon drifted off to sleep.

Early the next morning the train slowed down and Mike, who was already awake, got up and looked out of the door. Mike saw a sign coming up for Richfield, Utah. He went over and shook Reba awake as the train slowed down more.

"Looks like this train is going to stop, so we better get off when it gets slow enough," Mike said.

"Good deal; I am getting hungry anyway," she replied.

The train continued to slow and, when it was barely moving, they exited the boxcar with their bags.

Moving across the tracks and into the town, they found a restaurant. After refreshing themselves and having a good meal, they headed back to the tracks. Choosing the tracks that headed southwest, they set out walking in that direction. About a mile outside of the small town, near the tracks, was an abandoned building. They walked over and sat down in front of the building and waited for the train to come along.

After waiting for an hour, they finally saw the train moving in their direction. They slipped around the corner of the building, out of sight. Mike peeked around the corner and watched the train and, when it got close to the building, he ducked back beside Reba as the train passed by. Soon the boxcars were in sight, and they moved over close to the train, which was gaining speed. When they hopped onto the boxcar, they felt it was a good choice as it had some straw in both ends and was otherwise reasonably clean. Placing their bags in one end, they took their positions at the door and watched as the train's speed increased. Once again, they were on their way.

In a couple of hours, they crossed the tip of Arizona and headed into Nevada, across the Indian reservations, and toward Las Vegas. Later on, moving southwest, the train slowed down as it approached Las Vegas. Mike and Reba thought about getting off in Las Vegas, but that idea was changed when the train picked up speed while passing the city, and was quickly at full speed as it raced into California.

The hair on the back of Mike's neck stood up, and he got chill bumps, when he saw a sign indicating California. "Reba, we are in California!" he exclaimed, as he reached over and put his arm around her while holding the doorframe with the other hand.

"Yes, isn't it exciting!" she replied.

They were both young and full of dreams. Reba had dreams of becoming an actress, but Mike didn't know what kind of work he would pursue. He was open to a variety of jobs and would consider his options when the opportunities came along. Mike was certainly physically fit, which opened up opportunities for the construction trades, and he was mentally capable as well. They were both healthy young adults, very happy to have found each other and to receive support of each other through this enjoyable and exciting journey across the country. Reba was grateful that Mike was there and helped her through her time with the surgery and her recovery. As the days passed by, they had become more bonded together.

They were moving now into unknown territory, full of life, with ambition and desire to make their marks and to get ahead in life. It was a very exciting time for them both as they looked to the immediate future with anticipation.

Now they were moving into a place where they had only dreamed about, or read about in magazines. Both Reba and Mike had come from a somewhat small place in central West Virginia. The cities they were now maneuvering through were foreign territory to them, and it would take some time to adjust and learn how to get along. Their new surroundings offered challenges they had never encountered before. Not that they were fearful, but they were a little apprehensive and somewhat overwhelmed with the prospect of moving in and around Los Angeles, and the other large cities unfamiliar to them. Whatever happened in the future, they planned to face it together, and that reassured them both.

They were quickly approaching San Bernardino and decided to leave the train at that point. They sat poised at the door, with their bags by their sides, as the train began to slow down. With the train slowing more, and barely moving, they slipped easily to the ground, pulling their bags with them. After crossing several railroad tracks, they soon were walking toward the center of the city. They found a decent looking place, called "The Downtowner Restaurant," and entered. Mike waited as Reba freshened up and, when she returned to the booth, he took his turn to wash up.

After his visit to the rest room, Mike returned to the booth and slid in opposite Reba. The waitress arrived and they ordered their meal.

"What do you say we just find a place to spend a couple of nights to unwind and look around and get our footing?" Mike said, looking over at Reba.

"That sounds good to me; I'd like to soak in a tub of hot water for about an hour. That last stretch seemed like a long one to me." She smiled at him.

"Yes, it was a long one, and I think it would do us good to just relax and get accustomed to not moving for a while. We can do a little sight seeing too."

The waitress brought the food, and they leisurely enjoyed their meal. When they had finished eating, Mike paid the check, and they exited the restaurant while walking out onto the street. Standing in front of the restaurant, they looked both ways, trying to decide which way might be more promising to them. Deciding to go west, they turned left, and started slowly walking down the street.

The warmth of the California sun warmed their faces. It was a clear day with the sky filled with puffy white clouds that resembled big, white, cotton balls.

As they walked leisurely down the street, Mike noticed a used-car lot on the corner across the street.

"Let's go over and look at the cars," he said, pointing across to the lot.

They strolled over and started to look at the cars.

"May I help you folks?" said the short man in the plaid coat, walking toward them.

"We were just looking at the cars you have here," said Mike.

"Okay, take your time. If I can help you, I'll be over by the office."

"Thanks," said Mike.

They looked around a while and spotted a blue 1946 four-door Plymouth, for the price of $350.

"What do you think, Reba? We are going to need to get around someway."

"Yes, we are. It looks clean, and it is very pretty. I like it, Mike."

Mike walked over and talked to the man and, in a few minutes, he returned with the key and a dealer's tag.

"Let's take her for a spin," he said, holding the door open for Reba.

Soon they pulled out onto the street and were driving down the street.

"Hey, not bad! She runs real good, and smooth too," said Mike.

"Yes, it is very comfortable. It's nice, Mike."

They circled the block and returned to the dealer's lot.

"Well, what do you think?" asked the salesman, as they got out of the car.

"I think we'll take it," said Mike.

"Fine; just fine," beamed the little man.

"Come right into the office, and we'll write it up, sir. It won't take long."

The little salesman was right, it didn't take long, and they were going down the road in their blue Plymouth with the temporary tag on it. Pulling in at a service station, Mike filled the car with gas.

"Where do you want to go, Reba?" asked Mike, as he slid in under the steering wheel.

"Let's go to Hollywood," she smiled at Mike.

"Look out Hollywood, hear we come," said Mike as they pulled out onto the road.

Down the road they went toward Los Angeles, and on to Hollywood. In the thick of the traffic, they spent several hours touring around, looking at the studios and mansions where the "stars" lived. It was a whole new world for both of them, and they took it all in as they moved along speechless and awestruck by the magnificence of the estates.

As the day wore on and the sun began to set, they found themselves near Long Beach and decided to stay there for the night. Checking into the Rainbow Motel, they unpacked the car and moved their belongings into Room Number 10.

It had been a long day, and Reba showered first while Mike lay on the bed, watching TV. When she came out of the shower, he went in.

After changing into fresh clothes, they walked down the street to Millers Restaurant and enjoyed a good meal.

Then they headed for the beach and walked for a while along the edge of the water, listening as the waves crashed along the shore. They walked a long distance down the beach and then turned and walked back to the motel.

They were both very tired and soon turned in for the night.

The night passed quickly and, at 8:00 A.M. the next morning, they were up and on their way to Millers for breakfast. After breakfast they picked up a newspaper and returned to the motel. With a couple of hours before checkout time, they both read the paper. Reba was looking for studios wanting actresses, or any possibilities for auditions. Mike was looking for employment opportunities, but didn't find much.

With the arrival of checkout time, they loaded the car and were off to the center of the city, with Reba holding the newspaper. She had spotted an address of an agent who was advertising for actors.

They soon found the agent's address and parked the car near the building along the street. Climbing the steps to the second floor, they went into the agent's reception room.

Mike waited and leafed through a magazine as the secretary escorted Reba back to the agent's office. It was an older building, but the interior looked new and modern, apparently having been refurbished recently.

In about thirty minutes Reba came through the office door with a dark-haired man following her.

"Hi, I am Sydney Jefferies, and you must be Mike?"

"Yes sir, Mike Clark."

"Reba told me some about you and about your trip out here to L.A. That was some trip you had!"

"Yes, it was quite a trip," said Mike.

With that, they shook hands and Reba and Mike exited the reception room.

"What did he say in there?" asked Mike.

"Well, he told me to stay in touch, that there was some walk-on parts coming up, and he could use me in those. He said I had the looks to make it, and recommended that I take acting classes. He gave me a brochure about a school I might consider. He said to let him know when we got settled with an address and phone number so he could reach me."

"That is really encouraging; maybe you will get some work soon." Mike said.

"Yes, it is exciting Mike, I could be in a movie soon; not a big part, but in a movie, nonetheless," Reba said, smiling at Mike.

"That is wonderful," Mike smiled back.

"In the meantime, we had better look for a place to stay," Mike said.

"Oh, Mr. Jenkins said to check out the Crawford

Hotel, and we might find something there that would suit us," Reba said. "Many aspiring actors have stayed there over the years, he said."

Pulling over to the side of the road, they checked the map and found they were not far from the Crawford Hotel. After turning left at the next intersection, they took a right onto 1ˢᵗ Avenue, the street where the hotel was located.

They quickly found the Hotel and were soon in the lobby, looking around. It was an older place, but very well preserved, and showed the good care it had received over the years.

After looking at their room, they decided to take it, for a month. They registered, then moved their luggage in and unpacked their belongings.

"It feels good to be settling in here, Mike, after being on the move so much," Reba said, moving her extended hand around the room in a sweeping motion.

"Yes, it sure does. Now we can relax and see what we can do here for a while. And, if we like it here, we will renew for another month. It seems to be convenient to everything we need, even a restaurant downstairs, off the lobby."

"Yes, which reminds me, I am getting hungry. What do you say I buy us lunch down there, and give the restaurant a try?"

"Sounds good to me; I'm getting hungry too," Mike replied.

They walked down to the restaurant and enjoyed their lunch. After lunch, they decided to go to the beach for the afternoon. Arriving at the beach, they took their shoes off and left them in the car. It was only a short distance down to the beach through the sand. Walking along in the surf, the water just covering their ankles, they enjoyed the afternoon and the beauty of the beach. They could see the sandy beach for miles in either direction. The beach was sparsely populated that day and not crowded at all. In fact, they would walk quite a distance on the beach before they would pass someone. It was nice there, being together and enjoying the warmth of the sun, tasting the salty air that the constant breeze of the ocean projected toward them.

They walked for miles down the beach, occasionally speaking, but more often communicating with exchanged glances, accompanied with a grin, or the squeezing of the hands, which remained locked together. Their entwined fingers were released only long enough to retrieve a special shell that washed ashore and was placed in Mike's pocket, and then their fingers were relocked.

Coming to a small cove, they decided to sit and rest a while there, in their own little hideaway.

It was very peaceful there, leaning against the bank behind them, with Reba up against Mike, his arm around her. They sat there a long time looking out to sea. A ship could be seen, off in the distance toward the horizon, and it seemed to get smaller and smaller. Reba soon drifted off to sleep, and Mike's eyes were heavy also. They continued to relax and listen, with their eyes closed, to the waves as they gently dropped against the shore. The flood tide was coming in slowly, and each wave brought the edge of the water closer to them. Reba continued to rest peacefully there with Mike's arm around her.

After relaxing for a while, Mike opened his eyes when he thought he heard voices. He slowly removed his arm, and laid Reba's head against the grass on the bank. He then got up and walked over to the edge of the little cove and peered over the edge of the bank. In the distance, he could see two men digging a hole, up near the bank, where the beach ends. One man was short and stocky, while the other was of medium build and tall with a mole on his left cheek.

Mike could see them clearly and stayed out of sight, watching as they dug the hole.

Once they had finished digging, they placed a small box in the bottom of the hole, which was some two feet deep. After filling in the hole, covering the box, they picked up their shovel and made their exit over the bank and to a green pick-up truck they had parked in the parking area. They put the shovel in the bed of the truck and left the area driving south.

6

J ust as they drove off, Reba woke up and saw Mike. "What are you looking at, honey?

"Come here, quick," said Mike, motioning with his finger. Reba hustled over beside Mike.

"See that green truck going down the road?" Mike said, pointing as Reba looked.

"Yes, what about it?" she asked.

"They just buried something over there by the bank. Let's go see what it is," he said.

They proceeded to walk over to the area and, finding a small board nearby, Mike began to dig where the men had just been. In a few minutes his board struck the metal box.

Continuing to dig, he uncovered the box. He pulled the box up out of the hole and opened it. Inside were four plastic bags of a white powdery substance that looked like sugar.

"What is it, Mike?" Reba asked, with wide eyes.

"I am not an expert at this, but I'd say it is drugs."

"Oh, Mike, what should we do?"

"I guess we had better report it to the police and let them handle it."

"Let's just put it back like it was for now and go to the police and tell them about it."

"Whatever you think, honey."

Mike quickly closed the box and, putting it back into the hole, he covered it up.

"Okay, let's see now, we are right across Beach road from that abandoned building next to the vacant lot, which is right by the Esso station on the corner," Mike said, as he mentally filed the location in his mind.

With that, they retreated back the same way they had come. It took a few minutes to reach the car, and they drove back down to the Esso station and called the police.

In a few minutes the police pulled up, and they told them all they knew about the buried box on the beach. After taking the information about where they could be reached, and all the information about what they had found, the police wanted Mike and Reba to escort them to the box of drugs, which they did. The police asked them to say nothing about it, and told them they would be in touch with them later. They said they would set up surveillance, in hopes of catching whoever picked up the drugs. The police said it looked like a drug drop-off point. Reba and Mike returned to the hotel. The police left to put the plan in motion, after determining that they would use the abandoned building to stake out the area.

Mike and Reba had no idea that two men followed them back to the hotel. They thought they had seen and watched everything, from the time the men had buried the box, until the police had left.

It had been a full day, and Reba decided to soak in a tub of hot water, while Mike lay down on the bed to watch TV. When she came out of the bathroom, Mike was asleep. She silently got into bed and, snuggling up to his back, she soon joined him in sleep.

Two days later, Mike noticed an article in the newspaper where two men had been arrested after they had retrieved the drugs, and were driving down the road. They thought that would be the end of that story.

Reba had enrolled in school, and was taking acting classes twice a week. During the day she talked on the phone to her agent, and called other agents as well. She had not made a commitment, so was free to go with whichever agent could get her work.

Mike hadn't found any permanent work, so he took a part-time job across the street from the hotel, in a place called "Jack's Place," which was a bar and grill with a couple of pool tables in the back. He was a part-time bartender, handy man, and kitchen helper. Whatever needed to be done, he was called on to do it. It was three days a week, and more if they called him. It was convenient, anyway, and he didn't plan to do it forever. Since it did provide some income, which they needed, he decided to stay there for a while and continue to look for something better.

That Saturday, after they had left a restaurant a couple of blocks from their hotel, Mike and Reba were going down the street window-shopping and enjoying the warmth of the sun.

As they walked along, Mike noticed a man and a small boy walking in front of them, some ten feet or so. The little boy looked to be seven or eight years old, and was tossing a basketball up in the air as they walked. He would toss it up and catch it, and toss it up and catch it, as they walked along.

"May be a basketball star in the making there," Mike said, grinning at Reba.

"Cute little fellow, with that dark hair," she said.

As they approached the intersection, the little boy tossed the ball and, when it came down, he missed it. As it fell, it hit the corner of the curb and bounced out into the street. The little boy took off after the ball, to retrieve it, giving no thought of the traffic.

The light changed to green, and the traffic began to come across the intersection toward the ball, just as Mike and Reba arrived behind the man.

"Mike, the little boy!" shouted Reba, with a distressed look on her face.

"Come back, Johnny!" the man yelled.

Mike had seen what was coming, and bolted immediately into the street, in front of the oncoming traffic, after the boy. Just in time, Mike reached the little boy and scooped him up in both arms, while his momentum carried him forward, racing safely to the other side of the street with the boy in his arms. The traffic quickly sped past, barely missing them. They heard the basketball pop and burst when it was crushed underneath a car. Mike carried the little boy to a bench across the sidewalk, in front of the building.

When the light changed again, Reba and the man came rushing over.

The man put his arms around Johnny and was very nervous as he sat beside the boy on the bench.

"Oh, Johnny, you could have been killed!" he exclaimed.

"I'm sorry, Grandpa," the little boy said, as he returned his grandfather's hug.

When they had calmed down somewhat, the man looked at Mike.

"Sir, you saved my grandson's life! Thank you so much! How can I ever repay you for what you did? You are a very brave man."

"I am just glad that I was able to reach him in time," Mike replied.

"I must repay you for saving his life. I am in your debt, sir."

"Oh no, I just did what anyone would do. You owe me nothing."

"No, please, I must do something for you. Please come to my house for dinner this evening."

Mike looked at Reba, who had joined him on the bench.

"We don't have anything else to do, we might as well," she said, as she answered the look on his face.

"Yes, we would be glad to join you for dinner, and thank you," said Mike, as he turned his attention back to the man.

"Very good then, my car is right around this corner.

We can go now," he said.

They followed as the man took the boy's hand and proceeded around the corner to his car.

Arriving at a new-looking blue four-door Cadillac, the man opened the front and back doors of the car near the curb. Johnny got up front, and Mike and Reba got into the back. When the man got into the driver's seat, he turned and reached his hand out to Mike.

"My name is Carl Davis, and this is my grandson, Johnny," he said.

"I am Mike Clark, and this is Reba Jefferies," said Mike.

Little did Mike know that his bravery would pay him unexpected dividends in his near future.

Mr. Davis drove down the road, soon crossing under Interstate 15, and headed East on the Interstate. When he got to Highway 395, he went north to Route 18 and turned west. About 5 miles down Route 18, he turned right and went up a long private road, lined on both sides with trees and flowers, which were obviously kept immaculately manicured.

"This is our place here, which began back at Route 18," said Mr. Davis.

"We have 150 acres here, counting the 20 acres over to the left, there in the comer, which we haven't worked in some time."

Reba and Mike sat silently as they took in the beautiful acreage before them.

They pulled around the circular drive in front of the huge house and stopped. Everybody got out of the car.

"Come in and meet the family," said Mr. Davis.

Mike and Reba followed Mr. Davis and Johnny into the house, and met the family, which consisted of his wife Jean, and Johnny's mother, Valerie, who was their daughter-in-law. Valerie, who had lived with her in-laws for several years, often referred to them as "Mom" and "Dad." Sally Valetta was the maid and housekeeper, and her husband, Jim Valetta, was the gardener and handy man. The Valetta's house was situated behind the main house, and was the servant's quarters. Donald Davis, Johnny's father, was not there at that time. He was in the fields with the men who were tending the crops. They were harvesting lettuce that day. Also, Carlos, who was the Valetta's ten-year-old son, was in the fields with Donald.

Carl immediately told them about Mike rescuing Johnny. As he was doing so, they all were looking Mike over while they nodded their approval. Everyone there was very friendly to Mike and Reba, and took them right in as one of their own.

When Carl finished with the introductions and telling his story, everybody went about their business and left him with his guests.

"Come with me, and I'll show you around," he said, walking through the house and out the back door. They walked across the big porch, which ran the width of the house and out into the back yard.

Reba and Mike admired the back yard, which was enclosed by a white fence with flower gardens placed in random fashion throughout. Each of the gardens was full of bloom, and bordered with good-sized rocks.

In the middle of the yard was a circular fountain with water squirting out of the mouth of a fish while standing on its tail. The fountain contained different varieties of large gold fish that were swimming around happily.

"What a beautiful place you have, Mr. Davis," said Reba.

"Thank you. It does keep Jim busy, since he does all the yard work, taking care ofthe flowers and everything," Mr. Davis said, directing them to the jeep parked beyond the gate in the back.

"Lets take a little ride, and I'll show you around the place," he said.

They all got into the jeep, and Mr. Davis drove them around the vast property. Mr. Davis told them how he had worked and built up his business by raising vegetables and fruit on the land. Each field was different in that it contained its own particular vegetable. Beyond the vegetable plots were the orchards and, beyond that, over the rolling hills, were the rows of grape vines in the vineyard. It was all beautiful and immaculately kept.

There were people working in the different fields, and quite a number of people working to harvest the lettuce. There were several service buildings at the end of the vineyard, some of them quite large. And, at the end of the vineyard, there were the wine presses in the winery.

Mr. Davis escorted them through the winery and down into the cellars where the wine was aging in the big barrels. It was cool down in the cellars. When Mr. Davis spoke of the wine, Reba and Mike could see the pride he took in the hard work he had put into the vineyards.

They continued their tour of the vast property. Mr. Davis told them the history of how his father had settled there before him and began to farm the land, which was purchased at a fraction of its present value. When his father died and left the estate to him, he quickly expanded the growing areas to produce more of a variety of vegetables and added the vineyard as well. The vegetables were trucked to wholesalers, who shipped them throughout the country. There was always a ready market for their products, and the business was steadily growing. Their wines had become quite popular throughout the country. Mr. Davis had expanded the vineyard once, and was thinking of expanding it again. There was not only a demand for his wines, but a good demand for the grapes as well.

His business was prospering, and he was always looking for good help to work in the fields. Many of the workers would work a while and then move on. There were quite a few who stayed somewhat permanently. However, with the rotation of the crops, they could go from one to another and have work enough for them. The workers lived in the barracks at the end of the property, which provided good housing for them. The housing and conditions were more reasons for the workers to remain there. Many of the farms, which they worked on, didn't compare with the amenities provided here on the Davis property. The good treatment and fairness of Mr. Davis had caused his reputation to spread throughout the workers, which helped the farm to flourish and to keep his employees there.

There was plenty of acreage left on the vast farm that was not being used which provided room for expansion in the future.

After the two-hour tour, they headed back to the big house.

Mr. Davis ushered them into his large study and closed the door. Seating himself in his big easy chair, he invited his guests to sit on the couch, which was covered with the same soft leather as his chair.

"Well, now that you have had the grand tour, what do you think of the place?" he asked, as he relaxed in his chair. His eyes went from one to the other as he studied them.

"It sure is a beautiful place, and you have so many different products. It's very busy out there," said Mike.

"Yes, we are growing. We stay very busy keeping up, as best we can, with the demand for our products."

"Now, it is your turn to speak. Tell me all about yourselves," he said, with an inviting smile.

For the next hour, they had a nice chat, and Mike and Reba told him how they had come to California. While telling him all about their adventures across the country, Mr. Davis listened intently. He was very much impressed that they would even attempt to do such a thing as that.

Sally served them iced tea as they continued to get acquainted.

They talked a while longer, and then Mr. Davis looked very seriously at them.

"Today, you ran out into the traffic and surely saved my grandson's life. Taking no thought for your safety, you ran for him and rescued him from the oncoming traffic. He would have been seriously injured, if not killed, had it not been for your brave act. I thank you, and I will be eternally grateful to you."

"I want to do something for you to show my appreciation and, in that regard, I am prepared to offer you a position here on the farm. I would like you to come and work here on the farm. Later on, if you like the work and all, then you would take charge of all the workers as my superintendent. You would be responsible for them in every way, from the hiring, to the firing, and to the supervision of their work. It is a big job, but I will pay you well, and you will find that they are not that hard to work with. After a period of adjustment and familiarity with the workers and the work itself, you will have full charge of the workers here, if you think the job is something that you would like to do."

"As for Reba," he smiled at her and continued," You could help Mike with the book work and be his assistant. You will receive an appropriate salary also. You would also have all the time you need to pursue your career. You both would be provided housing here in the upper level of the house. You each could have a room and, of course, take your meals, here with us. Whichever you choose, these things will be in accordance with your busy schedule."

"I just did what anyone would do, sir, and I am glad it turned out as it did for Johnny's sake. Mr. Davis, that is a very generous offer. I just don't know what to say."

Mike looked over at Reba and reached over to take her hand as if asking her to say something.

"You are a very generous man, Mr. Davis, and I would hope that our work would prove to be adequate for such an offer as you have just made," said Reba.

"I don't know how much I could do, actually, with going to night classes and, hopefully, finding some parts to perform in," she added.

"I am sure that, in time, you will catch on to the business and fit right in," he said. "As for the time, you can go and do at your own pace as little or as much as you want. There is no time schedule, but any work at all would help of course; however, you are to go at your own pace, no pressure at all. If both or one of you decide not to work here, that is fine, but the job is there for you, should you decide to accept it."

"Let me show you around the house and to your quarters, should you decide to stay," he said.

They followed Mr. Davis up the long circular stairway to the upper floor. Their quarters would consist of two large rooms. One of the rooms was a bedroom with a big bed and bathroom, off to the side, and walk- in closets on the other side. There was a big dresser and a mirrored-vanity dresser. End tables with matching lamps were on each side of the bed. The room was immaculately kept, and appeared to have recently been painted. The room next door had an adjoining door, as well as the door from the hallway. It was furnished with a large bed and a small desk, upon which sat a wide lamp, with a comfortable looking chair behind the desk. Along the wall there was a leather sofa and a chair, off to one side, in front of the desk. There were two big windows behind the desk, which allowed the light to fill the room to the degree that the draw-drapes were opened. Mike and Reba were very impressed.

"Perhaps later on, when you are more settled, you might prefer the little house down by the twenty acres in the comer of the property, but for now this should serve you adequately," he said.

"More than adequate, sir, this is fantastic," said Reba.

"Yes, it certainly is, Mr. Davis, but are you sure about this offer, sir?" asked Mike.

"Yes, I am quite sure. I wish you would give the offer a try, for a while anyway. If nothing else, just to see how you like it. If you decide not to stay after a time, then you would not be obligated to stay. The only contract we would have is our handshake."

Mike looked at Reba, who was smiling.

"Would it be all right if we stayed in town until our rent is up, and commute out here, since we are all paid up at the hotel? It would give us some time to get used to things," Mike asked.

"Yes, of course, How ever you want to work it," replied Mr. Davis. "Your rooms will be here for you if and when you want to stay. You can stay as little or as much as you choose."

"In that case, we accept your offer, and we thank you," said Mike, as he extended his hand toward Mr. Davis.

"Good, now let's have some dinner. Just come on down to the dining room when you are ready. I will go freshen up also, and see you there," said Mr. Davis, as he vigorously shook Mike's hand.

"Yes sir, we will be right down," said Mike.

CHAPTER

7

Mike and Reba freshened up and walked down the long stairway to the dining room. While they entered the room, Mr. Davis rose from his chair, indicating they would sit just to his right, as he held the chair for Reba.

They were introduced to Donald Davis, and they began to eat the delicious meal that Sally and Jean had prepared.

Sally helped serve the meal. She and her husband, Jim, had already eaten in the kitchen, and Jim had gone out to work on the flowers. Most of the time, out of respect, the Valetta's ate in the kitchen so as not to intrude on the family. Occasionally they would eat with the family and were always welcome to do so.

When Mike and Reba were introduced to Donald Davis, Mike recognized the mole on his left cheek, and was astonished to be looking at the man whom he had watched bury the metal box earlier.

Carl and Jean were very gracious people, treating the employees as family. They ran their business with an easy-going manner and had genuine concern for their employees. They often provided medical care for the employees when one of them became sick, not that they were obligated to do so, but out of the goodness of their hearts, and because they really cared about them.

Seated around the table was Mr. Davis at the head and next to him, counterclockwise, were Reba and Mike. Next to Mike was Johnny and at the opposite end from Mr. Davis, was Donald Davis, Johnny's father. Next to Donald was his wife, Valerie, and then Mrs. Davis.

The conversation was light and kept flowing while Mrs. Davis asked Mike and Reba many questions about themselves. They continued to get to know each other as Mike and Reba shared their experiences about coming across the country on the train. Mr. Davis announced that Mike had taken the job and would, hopefully, become his superintendent. He also told his family Mike and Reba would be staying there in the house, perhaps in the future.

Donald seemed in a hurry. He finished eating before the others, and excused himself by saying he had to go somewhere. Valerie followed him upstairs briefly, but soon returned to the table alone. After finishing the meal, they retired to the large denjust off the dining room. They chatted some more, and Mike and Reba shared more of their experiences coming to California. Mrs. Davis seemed pleased to have them there, and was quite taken with them both, expressing her admiration for the courage it took to come out there on the train. Valerie was friendly also, and entered into the conversation, asking many questions. Johnny went about playing on the floor with some toy vehicles while the adults talked.

The time quickly passed, and soon it was time for Valerie to send Johnny upstairs for his bath. She decided to call it a night also, and went up with him. Donald had been gone since just after the meal, and the Valettas had gone to their little house in the back. Mr. and Mrs. Davis said goodnight and went to their bedroom, which was on the first floor.

Mike and Reba walked outside and sat on the edge of the porch. It was comfortably warm, and the night was filled with the sound of crickets as the fireflies blinked at them.

"This has been quite a day, hasn't it? Mike asked.

"It sure has been a day to remember," Reba answered.

"Reba, Donald Davis is one of those guys who buried the drugs at the beach; I definitely recognized him and the mole on his face." Mike quietly said, as he looked intently at her.

"Are you sure, Mike?"

"Yes, I am absolutely sure it was him."

"Oh, my goodness, he must be mixed up in drugs?"

"Yes, apparently he is," answered Mike.

"What are we going to do Mike?"

"Nothing right now; lets just think about it a while and then decide after we have had time to think of what would be the best thing to do."

"Yes, I guess you are right," she said.

"The Davis family is very nice. You already have a job. Things sure have happened fast. I would kind of like to slow down for a day or so myself," Reba continued.

"Yes, I think that would be a good idea. Anyway, it will take a little while to get accustomed to the surroundings and the farm and everything. We are in no hurry, but I know you want to go to L.A. and Hollywood, eventually. We will just take it one day at a time, and we will get you there."

"It sounds exciting, but I am a little nervous about it really," she admitted.

"I think that it is natural for you to be nervous about going to Hollywood. This will be a big step for you. So many have tried breaking into movies before and met with failure."

"I know, Mike, and it is definitely a long shot, but I intend to give it a try. Not tonight though, because I am tired," she said through a yawn.

"Yes, I am beat; let's go up," he said, standing and gently guiding her to the door.

They silently climbed the stairs and went into their rooms. After showering, they went to bed and soon drifted off into a peaceful sleep in Mike's bed.

The next morning they woke to the chirping of the birds and the sun shining through the window. Sleeping in a good bed had refreshed them both. After getting dressed, they went downstairs, feeling re-energized and ready for whatever the world had to offer them.

As Reba and Mike entered the kitchen, Sally and Jean were there to greet them.

"Good morning, come and sit down for breakfast," Jean said, extending her hand to the chair by her. They joined her for breakfast as Valerie served them.

"Carl will meet you in the yard after breakfast. He wants to show you both around some more and have you meet the workers," Jean said.

After a big breakfast, they went to the yard where Mr. Davis met them, and they were off in the jeep to meet the workers. Most of them were Mexicans, and some were Oriental. They first met Jose Valence, who was the foreman for the men, and the one that Mike would deal with concerning the workers much of the time. Jose had been there with his wife and two children for many years and was a trusted friend of Mr. Davis, as well as a loyal employee. He and his family lived in a small house near the barracks where the workers stayed. He was a friendly man, and smiled easily as he met Mike. Mike liked Jose instantly, as did Reba. Mr. Davis informed all of them that Mike would be in charge after he had gotten used to the farm and how things run. He told them to look to Mike for direction, and to bring any problems that they had to him.

On the way back to the house, Mr. Davis looked somewhat pained as he said, "I might as well be honest with you from the beginning about my son, Donald. He didn't come home again last night, and that is becoming more of a regular occurrence lately. Donald is becoming more and more undependable. When he and Valerie were married eight years ago, they moved into the house with us, and Johnny was soon born. Everything was fine for about five or six years, but the last couple of years or so have been very difficult.

He seemed to have lost interest in Valerie, and in working here at the farm. Often, he goes out at night and not return. I sometimes think he is mixed up with a bad crowd or something, but I really don't know where he goes or what he does. I do know that he has been drinking more and more and not treating Valerie or Johnny with much regard. I have had to cover for him, concerning the men and his duties, and the men have come to resent him. He never had the title of Superintendent, as you will. It was just understood that he was the boss, and for quite a while that was fine. Mike, I really hope you will accept this job, and its responsibilities, as I need someone to take over these duties."

"Well," Mike said, "when I am settled in here and feel comfortable doing my work, I will do the best I can for you. I am glad you told us about Donald. You don't think Donald will resent my taking his job, do you?" Mike started to tell Mr. Davis about the box he saw his son bury, but then thought it best to say nothing.

"No, I don't think so; he is probably relieved to not have to deal with the responsibilities. He hasn't taken the job seriously for some time. His mind seems to be somewhere else and, a lot of the time, he is somewhere else," said Mr. Davis.

"I just don't want to be in the middle of anything, Mr. Davis," said Mike. Inwardly, he now felt he had already gotten into the middle of something, since he had watched his son bury the box.

"I understand, but there will be no conflict there, so don't worry about that," Mr. Davis reassured him. "The job is yours if you want it, and I am relieved to know you will consider it. I have enough to do with my duties of running the farm without looking after the men and the crops," he said.

That day, and as often as they could the rest of the week, Mike and Reba spent their time in the fields with the workers. Working along side of the workers gave them a good understanding of the work and an opportunity to get to know them better. They also toured the living quarters of the workers with Jose. Mike assured Jose that they would get started on replacing the kitchens and expanding the facilities. The workers got excited when they heard that improvements were going to be made for them. Mike had gotten off to a good start with the workers, and they seemed to like him right from the start.

Reba and Mike commuted to the hotel the rest of that week so that Reba could go to school at night when she needed to be there.

Toward the end of the week, Reba mentioned going into Los Angeles, for the weekend. On Saturday, they took off in the jeep and drove to the city. Mr. Davis had given them a map and instructions on how to get to Hollywood and, eventually, they found their way to the places they wanted to see. There was not much they could do on the weekend except tour around and get the feel of the place. They enjoyed being out together in the big city, going here and there, looking things over. It was quite different from the cities they had been in before.

"Mike, this is really a jungle out here. How will I ever find my way around?" Reba asked.

"It definitely is big, but eventually I suppose a person would learn their way around," he said.

"This is such a big step Mike, it is a little frightening to me," she admitted as she looked around.

"You will get used to it and, who knows, it just might work out for you."

"I hope so; it is a little bit overwhelming though at first.

"You will be fine," he reassured her.

They continued to tour around the vast city, driving past the big studio complexes, and taking in all the sights like two dry sponges soaking up water. They enjoyed a good meal in a nice restaurant and then toured around some more. They had seen some of the places on their previous outings.

After dinner that evening, Mike and Reba decided to head back to the farm. They shared their experiences with Mr. and Mrs. Davis, who listened intently.

"Perhaps Jose could accompany you on Monday, and you could go back and make some more inquiries at the studios and some agencies," suggested Mr. Davis.

"Jose is very familiar with the streets and could take you anywhere you need to go," he continued.

"Yes, that would be great," said Reba.

"In the meantime, I will look in the newspaper for more of the agencies, in case I missed some. I gave the other agent this phone number, and the number at the hotel, so I wouldn't miss any of his calls."

They talked a while longer, and then everyone turned in for the night.

The weekend quickly passed and, on Monday morning, Mike waved to Jose and Reba as they drove down the road to return to L.A. Reba had made some calls, and was anxious to get on with her adventure.

Mike returned to his duties in the fields with the workers. He was quickly getting the hang of the operation there and learning more each day about the business. The men liked Mike and worked well for him. He still maintained his job at Jacks' Place three days a week, and had not decided yet about taking the job full- time at the farm and living there.

Mike had wanted to work some each day on the little house, down in the somewhat isolated corner of the property, which was on about twenty acres of land, not being used. It was a sturdy frame house with beautiful hardwood floors inside. With a couple of the men assigned to start work on the yard and gardens surrounding the place, Mike set about to order shingles for the roof. The house had been vacant for some time, but basically was in good shape. With a little work, it would make a nice place where someone could live. It seemed a waste to just sit there vacant when it could provide a nice place for a family.

That afternoon, Jose returned and joined Mike in the fields and began to help with the work.

"Reba had an interview this afternoon with an agent and decided to stay in the hotel tonight, Mike," Jose informed him.

"Thanks Jose, I will call her later," he replied.

They continued to load the truck with vegetables and, by that evening, the truck was on its way to the wholesaler, packed full of fresh vegetables.

With their day's work done, they headed for the house to get washed up for the evening meal. After washing up, they joined Mr. and Mrs. Davis, Valerie, and Johnny at the table. Donald Davis had not been there for a couple of days now. He had been seen around there less and less lately.

After starting the meal, Mr. Davis looked at Mike.

"How is it going out there Mike?" he asked.

"Not too bad, really. We have started fixing up the little house, down in the corner of the property, and we are repairing the kitchens in the living quarters for the workers."

"Yes, that is very good; I know they will like that. It has been needed for some time."

The meal continued with light conversation.

Later that evening, when Mike was walking alone in the back yard, admiring the different varieties of the beautiful flowers, a voice came from behind him.

"Beautiful, aren't they?"

He turned around, and there was Valerie.

8

"Oh, Hello, Valerie! Yes, they are very beautiful and so many different kinds," he said, trying to hide the nervousness in his voice.

"Sorry, I didn't mean to startle you," she said.

"Oh, that's fine; glad to have your company. I was just admiring the flowers and the beautiful sunset. It really is such an outstanding view from here. Quite a gorgeous view of the fields and the vineyard, in addition to everything else."

"Yes, I often come here in the evening to watch the sunset and enjoy the view," she said.

Mike had not really noticed her before, but now he realized how beautiful she was with her dark hair blowing back from her face in the slight breeze. Although Valerie was about five years older than Mike and Reba, she did not look any older than them at all. She was wearing a loose-fitting white blouse, which could not hide her ample breasts. The blouse was tucked into her flowing skirt, which was yellow with little flowers on it. She looked absolutely radiant as hues of red from the sunset were cast upon her flawless complexion.

"Up until a couple of years ago, Donald and I have been very happy here," Valerie said.

"That must be very hard for you now, with Donald coming and going the way he seems to do," said Mike, not wanting to pry, but wanting to offer comfort for her.

"No one knows, Mike, just how hard it has been these last two years for me. Donald has left me alone so much of the time. If it had not been for Johnny, I don't know what I would have done. Donald has acted as if he doesn't care for me at all, and gives only a minimum of time to Johnny. I sometimes think he is trying to drink himself to death, plus he has a bad habit of gambling. I know he has been going to Vegas much of the time, when he is not here, because I have friends who have seen him there. It wasn't that I was spying on him; they just told me they had seen him. I don't know where he gets the money to throw away," she went on.

Mike stood and listened attentively as she relieved herself of the mental burden she had been carrying by herself.

As she had been talking, they had slowly strolled along to the back of the lawn and, arriving there, she turned to Mike.

"Oh my, I am rambling on, boring you, I am sorry Mike, I didn't mean to burden you with my troubles," she said.

"No, Valerie, please don't feel that way, I am glad to listen and let you talk; it doesn't cost anything to listen," he said, smiling at her.

"I must admit, Mike, it does make me feel better having gotten it off my chest. It is so good to talk to someone. You are very kind to allow me to unburden myself like that. I didn't even realize I was going on so, there for a while," she said, returning his smile as she looked up to him.

When she looked up, Mike noticed just how pretty Valerie was with those dark eyes sparkling and the last rays of the slowly fading sun reflecting on her face. Their eyes shared a moment locked together, and then they both hastily turned away.

"I think I will go in now and check on Johnny and get ready for bed Mike," she said, turning and walking toward the house. She walked a couple of steps and then turned and looked at Mike.

"Thanks for listening to me, Mike," she said, stopping and turning back around toward him. Once again, their eyes were locked together, and they allowed them to remain longer this time.

"You are most welcome. And, any time you want to talk, I will be glad to listen," he said, squarely meeting her gaze, feeling the same weakness in his knees and rush of excitement that he had felt the first time their eyes had met.

She reluctantly surrendered the gaze and turned and walked in the house, not looking back.

Mike's eyes remained fixed on her until she was in the house and out of sight.

He stood there a few minutes thinking about their talk, and then went into the house and to his room.

"Oh, I have to call Reba, " he thought, as he reached his room. He called her, but she did not answer when the operator rang the room, so he decided to shower and try her again later. After his shower, he lay down on the bed and turned on the TV. He watched a little while until he fell asleep. Mike woke up later when a noise on the TV startled him, and he looked at his watch. It was five minutes past midnight, and he thought he would try calling Reba again.

He called the hotel and asked for their room. The phone rang several times, and no one answered. He hung up the phone and walked around the floor, thinking. *"Wonder where she is and if she is all right. Think I'll call the hotel again. "* He called the hotel again and reached the clerk on duty, who said he had not seen Reba come in since he reported for duty at 11:00 P.M. Mike hung up the phone and sat on the side of the bed.

"I hope she is all right. I guess I can 't do any more tonight. " With that, he decided to go to bed.

Mike rolled over on his back and could see through the opened window that the moon was nearly full. In his mind, he replayed the events of his life since the day he hopped on that train in his hometown. His eyes got heavier as, in his mind; he progressed across the country, reliving the events as they occurred along the way.

When he progressed to the events of the evening just passed, he thought of Valerie just three rooms down the hallway. The feeling of excitement returned as it had been felt when they had looked into each other's eyes. He wondered, *"Valerie, are you, too, looking at the moon? What kind of feelings did you have in the lawn tonight when we were talking? Did you have the same feelings that I did?"*

His last thoughts were of Valerie as he drifted off to sleep.

Mike woke up the next morning about 6:30A.M. and thought of calling Reba, but decided to wait until later. After his shower and breakfast, he headed for the fields and found Jose and the workers already there. He greeted them and began working with them.

Later on that morning, about 11:00 A.M., Johnny came running down to the field with a note in his hand. Arriving there, he gave the note to Mike.

"Thanks, Johnny," he said, as he unfolded it and began to read the note.

"Dear Mike,

Please give me a call at the hotel between 11:00 and 12:00 today as I have to go out after that and don't know what time I will return. Thanks. Talk to you soon.

Love, Reba

"Come on, Johnny, I'll walk back to the house with you," Mike said, as he looked at his watch.

Arriving there, Mike called Reba from his room and got an immediate response. "Hello."

"Hi, Reba, this is Mike, what's up?"

"Hi, Mike, guess what, I have gotten a small part in a movie! Mr. Jenkins, the agent we went to see, got me a walk-on part in a movie, where I will be walking down the street in two places in the movie, and then in a bikini on the beach in another place in the movie. It isn't a big part, but they are going to pay me $1500 for doing it. And, it is a start. There might be a speaking part when I am on the beach. Mike, I am so excited!"

"That is great news, and I am really glad for you. I tried to call you last night," he said.

"Yes, I had dinner with the director of the movie and I was late getting back to the hotel."

"Oh, I see," said Mike, feeling something in the pit of his stomach he didn't understand.

"I wanted you to call now because I have to go to the studio and go over the part. And, later on, the director wants to take me to meet some people. He is really a big shot, and knows all kinds of people in this business. He thinks I have a good chance to make something of this. It is very exciting!" she said.

"What is his name, Reba?" Mike asked.

"His name is Joseph Maxwell, and has directed several movies," she said.

"Mike, I have paid the rent for another month at the hotel, so that is taken care of," she added.

"That's great. I don't know when I will be in there, because we are very busy with the crops coming in," he said.

"I understand, Mike, but I hope to see you soon. I do miss you, but I feel that I have to take advantage of this opportunity while I can." she said apologetically.

"Yes, I understand. You are doing what you came out here to do, so more power to you. Just be careful, and call me if you need me for anything," he said, getting that funny feeling in his stomach again.

"I will, Mike. Hope to see you soon. I have to go now and get ready," she said hastily. "Hope everything is going good with you," she added.

"Yes, everything is fine and I'll talk to you soon. Be careful."

"I will. Bye, Mike."

"Okay, bye," he said.

Mike hung up the phone and, after going to the bathroom, he walked down the stairs, heading toward the back door, to go back to work, when he looked at his watch and realized that it was lunch time.

"Hi, Mike," he heard, as he walked past the kitchen door, returning to go to the dining room.

"Oh, Hi, Valerie, how are you doing today?" he inquired, looking in the doorway.

"Doing well thanks; lunch is ready," she said, smiling at Mike.

"I am ready for it, too," he said.

Mike went into the dining room and joined the family taking his place just to the right of Mr. Davis.

The usual greetings and small talk prevailed at the table as they enjoyed the meal that had been so expertly prepared for them.

Mike had gained a little weight; however, it was all muscle. He was well tanned, handsome, and in excellent shape. The work on the farm had been good for him.

During the meal, Mike and Valerie exchanged glances, which went undetected by the others. Donald was not there, and had not been there for several days. Nothing was said about him, or his absence.

The meal was soon over and Mike, on his way out the back door, turned briefly to steal another glance at Valerie. Finding that her eyes had found his first, Mike hastily exited the house and headed for the field, feeling the warmth of his cheeks and a thousand butterflies in his stomach.

The afternoon passed quickly and, before he knew it, he was on his way back to the house, having completed another day's work.

When Mike got to his room, he showered and lay down on the bed in his shorts to rest before dinner. He had worked hard all week. Tomorrow, on Thursday, the week's work on the farm would be finished. Friday would be the only day this week Mike would work at Jack's Place, in the city. He had arranged time away this week in order to help in the fields. The celery, radishes and peppers were all ready for harvesting, and they needed all the help they could get.

Mike fell asleep and was awakened by a small knock on the door.

"Mike, dinner is ready," Johnny called.

"Okay, Johnny. I fell asleep. I'll be right down."

Mike hustled into the bathroom to smooth down his hair and slip on clean jeans and a pullover red shirt. He soon was dressed and hurried downstairs, finding everyone already at the table.

"Sorry I was late; I slipped off to sleep," Mike said, offering an explanation.

"Aw, that's fine, Mike; we just started," said Mr. Davis.

Mike glanced at Valerie, and noticed that she looked flushed and her eyes looked swollen like she had been crying. She did not look at Mike, or anyone for that matter. Something was wrong, and Mike could sense it.

It seemed unusually quiet at the table, and the absence of the usual small talk was conspicuous.

"I wonder what has happened? Mike thought, as he looked around the table at the different faces. They all concentrated on their plates before them. Only Johnny appeared as his usual self, as he swung his legs playfully and smiled at Mike when he looked at him.

"Something is not right here, " he thought.

Soon the meal was over and they all left the table. "Mike, can we take a little walk together, I want to talk to you," Mr. Davis said to Mike in a low voice that only he could hear.

"Sure, I'll meet you out back," Mike answered.

"No, let's go to the front, I think the girls have gone out back," he said.

"Yes, that's fine," Mike moved through the front door and out onto the lawn in front.

As they walked to the fountain in the middle of the lawn, Mike wondered what was going on.

"Mike, I am sure you felt the strain of everyone at the dinner table, and I wanted to give you some explanation," the gracious gentleman began.

"Yes sir, everybody seemed a little uptight tonight, I noticed." The more Mike was around Mr. Davis, the more his admiration and respect for him grew.

"To get right to it, we had a call this afternoon from

Donald. He talked to Valerie first and left her in tears, and then I talked to him. I think Valerie has decided that enough is enough and will file for divorce. She is in the process now of contacting a lawyer that we have used in the past, and is starting the process. This has been coming for a long time, over two years now," Mr. Davis said, as he paused, and shook his head.

"I am sorry that things have gotten to be in such turmoil for you and the family, Mr. Davis," said Mike. "Yes, and I am too, but that is not the worst of it," he continued.

"Donald is in deep debt to someone and says he must have twenty thousand dollars right away in order to clear it up. I can't keep handing him money as I have done in the past. I am really at a loss as to what the best move would be," he said with a perplexed look.

"But that is not your problem; I will decide by the weekend; but I did want you to be aware of why the family is upset. It certainly has nothing to do with you, and I wanted to assure you of that. You have relieved my mind of a lot of stress with your working to keep the fields producing and getting the crops to market. At least I don't have to worry about that."

"If I can help in any way, I would be glad to sir; just tell me what you want me to do."

"Thanks, Mike, that means a lot, I will remember that."

9

After their talk, Mr. Davis bid Mike a good evening and returned to the house. He said he had some work to finish at his desk before he turned in for the night.

Deciding to take a walk, Mike proceeded to walk around the house, out the back gate, toward the fields. Everyone else had returned to the house.

"What a mess things have gotten in for the Davis family," he thought as he slowly and aimlessly walked. *"I feel somewhat responsible for it since I was the one to discover the drug-filled metal box Donald had buried. Now Donald needs twenty thousand dollars. Wonder where he got the drugs in the first place?*

Mike had a lot of questions and few answers, so he let it pass and tried to think about other things. The sun was all the way over the horizon now, but it was still somewhat light from the moon.

His thoughts turned to Reba and he missed her. He hadn't seen her since the first of the week, and tomorrow was Thursday. Thinking about the week being almost over, Mike realized this was the longest time they had been apart since they met on the train. Things had happened very fast in her career, and he hoped she was all right. He had only talked to her a couple of times that week and she sounded okay, but he couldn't help being be concerned. He cared deeply for her and felt responsible for her, even if they were not married.

"What about this guy, Maxwell, the director?" Mike pondered to himself *"Well, we are not married, so she can do as she pleases really,"* he thought. *"He better not hurt her though. Well, what if he did, I don't have any right to say anything. They have been spending a lot of time together apparently, meeting people, and who knows what else. I wonder if they ... if they have ..., no surely not. I have no right to even suspect anything like that. I'm sure she cares about me. Some of those guys are fast talkers, though. What about me? I have the same rights as she has. We are not married. I wish I had a drink! What about the way I have looked at Valerie, and she is a married woman!"* Mike felt guilty for his thoughts of her the past few days. *"Her marriage is over though, and didn't she look at me with wanton eyes as I did her?"* he thought, attempting to justify his actions. But he had not convinced himself fully that his actions were all right. He still felt guilty. *"I sure could use a drink, "* he thought.

Just then the wind picked up and it started to get dark quickly because of the black clouds overhead. They were now blocking the moonlight, and it had started to sprinkle.

Mike made his retreat back toward the house, but he had walked so far that the rain caught him before reaching the back gate. By the time he reached the back gate, the torrential rain had soaked his clothes through to his skin, and they hung on him like weights. He trudged on through the gate and to the house.

When he got on the porch, he removed his shirt and wrung the water out of it. He wondered what he would do, since he didn't want to track water all the way upstairs with his jeans dripping water.

"Here, Mike, take those clothes off and wrap up in this towel," he heard coming from the back door.

He turned, and there stood Valerie with a big beach towel.

"Thanks Valerie, did it ever come down!" he said.

"It came up so fast that I couldn't make it back in time."

"I know, that is the way it does at this time of year; it won't rain long, but comes up very fast," she said.

"I'll go on in and let you change, just leave the clothes by the door, and I will put them in the washer," she said.

"Okay, and thanks, Valerie."

With that, she was gone. Mike slipped over by the wall and removed his jeans and shorts. After removing his socks and shoes, He draped the towel around him, then piled the soggy clothes by the door and went in the house.

When he got inside, he saw Valerie standing in the doorway of the den, across from the stairway.

"Can I buy you a drink, Mike?" she asked. "I would love one," he said.

"Let me go up and get some clothes on and I'll be right back. Make mine brandy, if you will," he added. "You've got it," she said.

Mike went upstairs and dried off quickly and got dressed. When he returned, Valerie handed his drink to him.

"I have taken care of the clothes," she said.

"Thanks, Valerie, I appreciate it. This drink tastes good."

"I expect it would warm you up after getting caught in that downpour as you did."

Valerie had apparently just bathed, and her hair was pulled back and tied with a red ribbon. She was wearing a silk robe of a beautiful cream color. She was seated in a high-backed chair, facing the sofa. Mike took a seat on one end of the sofa facing her.

"I must say you look much better now than you did at dinner."

"I know Mike; I didn't feel very good then. I am slowly reconciling myself to the facts of life and what must be done. Dad told me that he had spoken to you about what was going on," she said.

"Yes, I hope you don't mind."

"Oh no, I don't mind, because you had to find out sooner or later, and you were already aware of the situation here. Actually, I am glad that he told you," she said, taking a sip of her drink.

"I am sorry you have to go through with the hassle of a divorce, but apparently you must." Mike didn't know exactly what to say to comfort her, but he wanted to say something.

"Yes, Mike, it has been coming for a long time. I put it off for as long as I could, but it is time to accept it now."

Valerie looked much better now, more relaxed, with a relieved look on her face. Of course, the drink had relaxed her some, too, and was beginning to relax Mike.

"Can I fix you another drink, Mike?" Valerie said, rising and walking toward him.

"Yes, that hit the spot, I will have one more, and then off to bed," he said, handing her the glass.

"Another day in the fields tomorrow, and then to Jack's Place on Friday," he said.

"Oh yes, I know that place, it's on Third Street, isn't it?"

"Yes it is, and across from the hotel where we rented the room," Mike said.

"I also have to go into the city on Friday, to see the lawyer," she said, as she handed Mike his drink and took a seat at the other end of the sofa. Both of them were half turned so they could see each other when they talked.

"How is Reba doing, Mike?" she asked.

"She seems to be doing fine as far as I can tell; I haven't seen much of her this week. She got a small part in a movie and she was very excited about that. She is being kept really busy now, with going to the classes and all." Mike took a sip of his drink.

"I hope to see her Friday when I go into the city to work," he said.

"She is a beautiful girl, Mike; I hope she does make it in her career. Wouldn't that be something?"

"Yes, it really would, but I kind of worry about her in there by herself. It would be easy for someone to take advantage of her," he said.

"Yes, it sure would. It has happened to so many young girls. They come out here with high hopes and good intentions, and some of them end up on drugs, or on the street, or dead. It is really awful with what some of them have to go through. I hope she steers clear of the scum that is part of that movie industry and is fortunate enough to go on and make her career the way she wants to." Valerie took a sip of her drink.

"Yes, I hope she will be all right in the midst of all those people. It is really a jungle in the city." Mike finished his drink.

"I think I am going up to bed now Valerie; thanks for the drink. If you get time, come by Jack's on Friday and I'll return the favor," Mike said, holding up his glass and smiling.

"Thanks, I might do that," she said, returning the smile and standing up, as she reached for his glass.

When she took the glass from Mike, she looked up into his eyes and smiled.

"Thanks for the good company and listening to me again, Mike."

"Any time; and thanks to you for the towel and drinks," he replied, as he walked to the door.

"No problem, goodnight, Mike." Valerie walked down the hall toward the kitchen with the glasses.

Mike went upstairs to his room where he got undressed, went to the bathroom, then to bed. He lay there on his back and listened to the rain, which was falling softly now. In a few minutes he heard a door close down the hallway. It had been quite a day, a very busy and eventful day.

He was worried about Reba. *"Maybe I should call her, "* he thought. He looked at his watch; it was ten minutes until midnight. *"This evening has flown by,"* he thought.

He dialed the hotel and asked for Reba's room. He let the phone ring several times, but there was no answer. Returning the phone to its cradle, he lay back down. *"Wonder where she is,"* he thought. *"I'll bet she is with that guy, Maxwell, again. I'll call her tomorrow and see if she is all right. Nothing more I can do tonight. "* His eyes soon became heavy, and he fell into a deep sleep.

The next morning, after they had worked a couple of hours in the fields, Mike walked to the house and called Reba. There was no answer, so he returned to the fields to work.

"I suppose she is busy at the studio or off shopping or something, " he thought. *"I will try calling her again later this evening."*

Mike did call her later that night, but again, there was no answer. *"Maybe I'll go by the room tomorrow and see her then, "* Mike thought. *"Surely she is all right. I hope so anyway.*

Mike was concerned about her, and he missed her very much. He slept fitfully that night.

He awoke and, after showering and dressing, he went downstairs to the kitchen.

"Good morning, Mike. Come and have some coffee, and I will fix your breakfast," said Sally.

"Thanks Sally; just coffee for me. I want to get into the city early," Mike said.

"The bacon is ready. It won't take a minute to fix the eggs. Are you sure you won't eat?" she persisted.

"Well, okay, I am kind of hungry. Thanks, Sally."

"Good, it won't take me a minute," she assured him. Mike ate the big breakfast that Sally prepared for him. He was just about to go out the front door and be on his way, when he heard from the stairway, "Morning, Mike."

He turned, and it was Valerie, wearing the same robe she had worn last night when they had their drinks together. She looked radiant to him with her hair fixed to perfection and her face glowing.

"Good morning, Valerie, I was just about to leave."

When Valerie looked at Mike she sensed that something was wrong. His eyes were blood-shot and he looked tired.

"Mike, are you okay?" she asked, moving toward him a couple of feet from the bottom step.

"Oh yes, I am fine; talk to you later," he said as he opened the door.

"Okay, Mike, have a nice day. See you later," she said, but she was not convinced that he was fine. He looked unhappy to her, not to the point of disconsolation, but worried. Her womanly perception had revealed it to her. city.

Valerie headed for the kitchen, and Mike drove to the Arriving there, he parked his car behind Jacks Place, in the parking area for the employees. He walked down the alley and across the street to the hotel.

He waved to the man behind the front desk and, not waiting for the elevator, he bounded up the stairs and went to the room.

She was not there. Mike stood just inside the door and surveyed the room. The first thing he noticed was a vase filled with long-stemmed red roses on the dresser. The bed was made up neatly, but scattered on the bed were some empty shoeboxes along with other boxes from different department stores. As he moved into the room, the presentiment he felt was overpowering, and only intensified when he reached the dresser. On the dresser in a tray were several pieces of jewelry which included gold earrings, bracelets and rings, some with stones and some without stones, but all beautiful. In another tray were several gold necklaces.

Mike picked up the card that was stuck in the flowers and read it.

"Hi, enjoyed the dances we shared and looking forward to the weekend, Joe."

Mike's knees got weak as he returned the card to its holder. He backed away from the dresser and sat down on the corner of the bed and continued looking around the room, feeling emptiness inside as the foreboding feeling intensified. As his eyes scanned the room, they soon found the opened closet. Mike looked at the beautiful dresses and skirts that hung there, along with the new blouses and scarves, none of which he had seen before.

Mike felt like a stranger in his own home. He suddenly felt very alone. A feeling he had never felt before swept over him like a wave of weakness, and an ache deep in the pit of his stomach.

He sat dejectedly on the corner of the bed and relived the trip out there on the train with Reba. He missed her terribly. He wanted it to be as it had been with her before, but the persistence of the ominous feeling had him convinced that it was not going to be that way again. He could perceive that with his mind and understand it, but his heart was having a hard time reconciling to the unwanted facts of the situation and to the events that were occurnng.

Mike sat there a while and then, looking at his watch, realized it was time to leave the room and walk across the street to Jack's Place.

CHAPTER

10

I t was 11:00 A.M. and the crowd was light when Mike took his place behind the bar. Both pool tables in the back were busy, but the regular customers were still at their places of work and had not yet arrived.

Mike, putting his feelings on hold, had recovered his composure somewhat, and was hoping the activity at Jack's Place would take his mind off of his troubles, temporarily at least. He began to stock the beer cabinets and serving the people at the bar as needed. The physical activity was a welcomed relief from the mental anguish he had just experienced, and very therapeutic for him. He went about his duties energetically and with purpose.

In the early afternoon business picked up. Mike was kept busy taking care of the customers at the bar, as well as filling the orders for the two waitresses who were waiting on the booths and tables.

It was 3:00 P.M. when Mike saw Valerie come through the door. She was dressed in a blue suit, which accentuated her curves perfectly. She looked gorgeous, and Mike noticed the customers' heads turning as she moved to the bar stool at the end of the bar.

"Hi, Mike," she said, smiling at him.

"Hi, Valerie," he said, as he walked over to where she was and returning the smile.

Mike leaned across the bar and whispered to her.

"Valerie you look gorgeous, and I think you turned every head in here."

"Thank you, Mike. How about that drink you promised me?"

"You bet, what will it be? It's nice to see you, Valerie."

"It's nice to see you, too. How about a Margarita?"

"One Margarita coming right up," he said, moving off to make the drink. Mike returned with the drink and set it in front of her on the bar.

"Mike, I sensed that something was wrong this morning. I don't mean that in a prying way, but just out of concern for you," she articulated.

"Well, yes, I am going through a bit of a time right now, but it will pass. It is nice to have someone concerned about me, though," he looked at her and gave a quick smile.

"It's Reba; apparently I am losing her, or have lost her. I was over at the room, and she has roses, and clothes, and I haven't talked to her, and oh, I don't know. Too much to go into now, I guess."

"I'm sorry, Mike, I am really sorry that you are being hurt. I knew that something was wrong from the look on your face this morning."

"Well, I really won't know anything until I talk to her, but the indications tell me that she must be getting very thick with this guy. Apparently, from what I can perceive, they have made some arrangements for the weekend. Just what, I don't know." He paused.

"Be right back," he said, as he took a beer to a guy sitting about halfway down the bar. Valerie tilted her glass for a sip, but her eyes followed him.

Mike returned to where Valerie was seated.

"How about you; how was your morning?" he asked. "I saw the lawyer and we had a long talk. He is starting the divorce procedure. I told the lawyer I don't know where Donald is, but that he spends a lot of time in Vegas," she said, pausing to finish her drink. "Care for another one?" Mike asked.

"Yes, thank you, you make a very good Margarita, Mike," she said, sliding her glass across the bar to him.

"Mind if I join you?" his eyes found hers and stayed there.

"I would love it," she said, not flinching at all.

Mike went to make the two Margaritas and thought he felt a smile following him. Chancing a glance, as he made the drinks, her smile confirmed what he had thought. He quickly turned his eyes back to the drinks as her smile widened. He soon returned with the two drinks.

"Here we are; what shall we drink to?" he asked.

"Be right back," he said, as he delivered a beer to another guy, and then another one to someone else.

Having fulfilled his duty, he returned to Valerie. "Okay, where were we?" he said.

She raised her glass slowly and looked into Mike's eyes.

"Our troubles are contemporaneous," she said.

"Here is to Mike and Valerie, and the future," she said.

"Yes, I agree, here is to us," he said, and they both drank.

After that drink, Mike made them another one, serving customers as needed.

"I suppose I had better make this one the last one Mike, since I have to drive home," she said, not looking up from her drink.

"I suppose so," said Mike, looking dejected with a far-off look in his eyes.

Valerie detected the look, and correctly interpreted it. "I wish I didn't have to go," she said, trying to comfort him, as she knew he was hurting over Reba.

"I wish you didn't as well, but I suppose you must," he conceded.

"How late do you work tonight, Mike?" she asked.

"I'll be here until midnight," he said apprehensively. Valerie meditatively sipped her drink.

"Are you all right, Mike?" she asked, genuinely concerned for his well being.

"Oh, yes, I am fine." He tried, unsuccessfully, to sound convincing.

"Excuse me a minute," Mike said, as he moved down the bar and waited on some customers.

Valerie's perception had revealed something entirely different from his answer. She knew he was hurting, and she wanted to comfort him. She knew, too, that her troubles were different from his. Valerie's troubles had come to a head after they had been brewing for a long time, and she was relieved that the divorce process had now begun. It was a great weight removed from her shoulders. Mike's troubles came up quickly, and he hadn't had time to reconcile himself to what had happened, or what he thought was happening. He was square in the middle of his problems.

Valerie felt that Mike was vulnerable in that condition, and was afraid he might do something rash. He might get hurt or hurt someone else. Anything could happen, and she didn't want anything bad to happen to him.

Mike returned to where Valerie was seated. "Where is the little girls' room, Mike?" she asked. "Just down the hall, on the right," he pointed down the hall.

"Be right back," she said. "Okay, I'll be here,"

When she returned to her barstool, Mike was waiting for her.

"Mike, I am concerned about you, and I really don't want to leave, but I have to be getting home now."

"I understand, and are you okay to drive?" he asked. She reached across the bar and put her hand on his, squeezing it tenderly, leaving it there while she spoke.

"I am fine, Mike. Will you call me later to let me know that you are all right?"

"Sure, I will call. I am fine; don't worry about me. You have enough to worry about," he said.

"Thanks for the drinks. I enjoyed being with you again, Mike."

"I enjoyed it, too, and be careful going home. Maybe you should call me to let me know you made it home okay?" he asked.

"Okay, I will do that. We are just two worriers, aren't we?" she said, smiling as she stood up and prepared to leave.

"Goodbye for now. I'll be waiting for your call," he said, as she walked toward the door.

She turned her head and mouthed the words, "Okay, bye," as she walked out the door.

Mike returned to his duties and removed the glasses they had used.

It was 7:00P.M. when the phone rang at the bar.

Jack, the owner, had just come in to help out as the crowd picked up in the evening. Jack answered the phone.

"Mike, it's for you," he called out in his gravelly voice.

"Okay; coming," Mike answered, thinking, *that must be Valerie, calling to say she made it home,* as he walked to pick up the phone from the counter where Jack had laid it.

"Hello?"

"Hello, Mike, this is Reba," was the reply. "Oh, well hello, this is a surprise!" Mike said.

"Yes, I guess it is, Mike. We need to talk. There are some things we need to discuss," she said.

"Do you mean on the phone, or in person?"

"I'd rather talk to you in person, if we could," she said.

"Yes, I'd like to talk to you, too, when did you have in mind?"

"I'll be at the room for about an hour to pack to go out of town. I should be there at eight o'clock, could you come over there for a while? I'll only have an hour, but I need to talk to you. I'll be coming over in a cab."

"We are very busy, but I can get away for a few minutes. Yes, I will be over there at eight o'clock."

"Okay, Mike, I'll see you at eight."

"Okay, see you then," Mike said, as they both hung up their phones.

In about five minutes there was another call, and Mike answered it.

"Hello, this is Jack's Place?"

"Hi, Mike, this is Valerie. I made it home fine."

"Good, I am glad," Mike said, "I just talked to Reba, and I am going over to see her at the room for a few minutes at eight o'clock. She told me she wanted to talk.

"Good Mike, I am glad you are going to talk with her. I think it will relieve your mind. I'll be here at the house if you want to talk later. Will you be coming home tonight?"

"I can't say anything for sure right now until I talk to her, but I definitely want to talk to her, and see what is going on. I think I know, but I am only guessing."

"Well, be careful, Mike, and call me if I can help, or if you need to talk to someone."

"I will Valerie, and thanks," he said. "Bye, Mike."

"Bye now, I'll talk to you later."

Mike went about his duties, glancing across the street now and then. At 7:50P.M. he saw a cab stop in front of the hotel and a woman get out, but he couldn't tell whether or not it was Reba. He waited until 8:00P.M. and called her room and, when she answered, he knew it was Reba he had seen leaving the cab. Then he talked to Jack and got permission to leave for a while.

He left the bar and walked across to the hotel. He didn't know what to expect. He had an idea, but he wasn't sure; he had no way to be sure. He was very anxious as he walked up the steps to the room. The adrenalin was flowing as he knocked on the door.

Reba opened the door.

"Hi, Mike," she walked over beside the bed. "Hi, Reba, what's going on?" he asked.

"Mike, you want to sit down and talk?" Reba was very nervous.

"There are some things that I need to tell you. I don't really know where to begin," she said.

"Just tell me what is going on," Mike said in an understanding voice.

Mike sat down in a high-backed chair, and Reba was sitting on the bed looking down at her folded hands in her lap.

"Mike, things have changed. And, they have changed so fast that I am not sure if I am doing the right thing," she began.

"I have met someone, and we have been seeing a lot of each other this week. He is real good to me; says he is crazy about me, and he is a very nice guy, and I kind of like him, too, and he has even said that he wants to marry me. I know it is too fast to think about marriage, but that is what he says. Look at all the stuff he has given me. He is loaded and all, not that it makes any difference, but he does have a lot of money."

"Is this that guy Joseph Maxwell?" Mike asked.

"Yes, it is him," she answered. "How old is the guy, Reba?"

"Well, he is a little older than me; he is forty-five," she said.

"He sure doesn't look it though," she hastened to add. "I thought you loved me, Reba," Mike stated in a quizzical manner.

"I do love you, Mike; I would do anything for you. I hate to have to tell you these things, but I must." Reba was obviously confused in the way she was talking.

"I just feel that I have to move on now. What we have, or had, was wonderful, Mike," Reba continued trying to explain, "but if I don't take the chance while I can, it might never come around again. And, Joe said he didn't want me to date anybody else now,"

"Is he saying what you are to do now?" Mike asked.

"No, I didn't mean that. It's just that he said if we were going to go together, that he couldn't go with someone who was going with someone else at the same time. You do understand, don't you, Mike?"

Reba had started to weep softly.

"Yes, I guess I do understand. I think you are rushing into this with this guy, but it is your life, and I don't have any right to try to stop you. I loved you very much, and still love you now; in fact, you are the only woman I have ever loved. I can't just turn it off like a faucet, Reba. The only reason I would try to stop you, or say anything, is because I am afraid that you will get hurt. I will probably always love you."

"I love you too, Mike, things have happened so fast. I sometimes wish the world would slow down a little. Things are just moving too fast for this country girl," she said through her sobs.

"That is just what I mean; you might be rushing when you need to slow down and think things through a little better," Mike said.

Reba had quit crying and stood up now.

"I have to get ready now, Mike. Joe and I are going to Vegas for the weekend." she said.

Mike's eyes got big, and she sensed what he was thinking.

"Oh, we haven't done anything yet, it wasn't that he didn't want to, but I mean we haven't yet, but we might this weekend. I was just trying to be fair with you, Mike."

"Well, it's bound to happen, if you are going to Vegas together; so I guess that's it for us then?" Mike said, looking at her.

"Just remember this, no matter what you do or where you go, if you ever get into trouble and need me to help you, just get the word to me, and I will come and help you, any where or any time. Never forget that. Go, Reba, just be careful, and take care of yourself," Mike said, while standing up, holding his arms opened toward her.

Reba rushed immediately into his arms. They embraced each other strongly.

"Oh, Mike, I thank you for loving me and helping me so much and for everything. Please don't hate me, Mike. I do love you," she said, with tears streaming down her face.

"No, No, I could never hate you; I will always love you. Remember, if you need me, you call or get in touch with me."

"Okay, Mike, and I will be checking on you. And, thanks, Mike."

They kissed as a token, not passionately as before, but affectionately.

"I had better get back to work; be careful," Mike said, as he walked out the door.

"I will, Mike. You take care. Bye now," Reba said. Absent of any hope whatsoever, Mike's head bent in despair as he walked down the stairs and through the lobby of the hotel. The gathering of the dark clouds overhead only contributed to his dejected mood and magnified the feeling of hopelessness that he was experiencing. He felt completely emptied by the news that she had found someone else and was so quick to give him up. It was hard for him to accept that she was gone and would not be coming back. It was as if someone, or something, had reached deep within him and tom away all of his insides, leaving him completely empty. He was so much in shock of what had happened that he blindly and aimlessly walked across the street in the direction of the bar. He wound up in front of his car in the alley, holding onto the front fender for balance. He was void of rational thinking at that time, as gloom settled over him, and loneliness took up residence in the place that only she had occupied before. He had grown to love her deeply over the short time he had known her, and it was his first love. Now it had quickly been tom from him, seeming to take a major part of him with it. He was numb with the despair that had replaced her. He remained there in the alley for a few minutes and tried to compose himself. When he felt that he was back in touch with reality, or reasonably so, Mike walked out of the alley and back inside. He took his place behind the bar. The bar was crowded now, and Jack was glad to have him back to help.

"Glad you are back, Mike, this place is hopping tonight.

"Say, are you all right, Buddy?" Jack thought he detected something askew in Mike's demeanor.

"Yeah, I'm fine, Jack," Mike lied, and went to get a beer for a guy at the bar.

Some would leave, and others would take their place. The bar stayed pretty full though, as it usually did on Friday and Saturday nights. Mike would make excellent tips tonight. He gave good service, and the guys tipped him good for the extra attention they received. A free drink for them now and then paid big dividends. Not only did Jack not care, he encouraged it. He had built his business on fairness and good service. A lot of the people were regulars who stopped in and had made Jack's Place their favorite watering hole.

The night wore on, and finally they closed the doors at midnight.

"Want a drink, Buddy?" Jack called to him from the bar, as Mike returned from locking the door and turning the open/closed sign around.

"Sure, why not, make mine bourbon and ginger," Mike answered.

Jack fixed them both bourbon and ginger.

Mike sat on a stool across from Jack who was behind the bar.

"You fix a good drink, Jack," Mike took a long pull on the drink.

"I've had a lot of experience, buddy," Jack smiled as he lifted his glass.

Jack reached over and picked up the cigar box behind him on the counter where Mike kept his tips and laid it on the counter in front of Mike.

"You must have had a good night, Mike?" Mike opened it up and counted it out. "Yeah, a good night; just over $225, Jack"

"Good for you, kid; you pulled a long shift for it; good for you."

Mike gave Jack a twenty-dollar bill. "What's this for?" asked Jack.

"I am taking a couple of bottles with me tonight when I leave."

Jack shoved the twenty-dollar bill back to him.

"Take what you want, Mike, but on me; you aren't paying for it. You are the best help I've ever had. I get it wholesale, anyway. Help yourself, buddy."

"I knew something was eating at you. Maybe you can drown it with bourbon; I never could; but I tried enough times. Just remember this; you have my home phone number if you need me." Jack was a decent guy and had become a good friend to Mike.

"I'm heading home to the little woman; you going to sweep up?"

"You bet, Jack, and thanks for everything. It's good to know you are there if I need you."

"No problem, kid, what are friends for?"

"Well, better get on home. Who knows, maybe the little woman is in the mood; I believe in miracles." Jack and Mike shared a laugh.

Mike finished his drink and locked the door behind

Jack. It took another hour to sweep up and get the place presentable to open up tomorrow. Finally his work- day was over, and he was beat. With the drinks and work, Mike was very tired. Mike got two bottles of bourbon and put them in a bag. He looked around, checking everything out.

He fixed the alarm and lights, and locked the door after going out. Walking down the alley, he got into his car and started to drive home.

It was a clear night with a full moon, just warm enough to be pleasant with a slight southwesterly breeze.

The dark clouds that were present earlier had all blown away, leaving the sky star-filled and clear.

By the time Mike got home it was 1:50 A.M. He went right up to his room, being as quiet as he could so he wouldn't wake anyone.

Mike was too tired to think or drink or anything. He went right to bed and was asleep in five minutes.

CHAPTER

11

Saturday morning arrived quickly, and Mike slept a little later than usual. He lay there a few minutes after he woke up and noticed the sun shining through the window as the sheer curtains fluttered in the warm breeze. Deciding to get up, he headed for the shower. After breakfast, which Sally prepared for him, he headed for the field. Seeing the workers had already started with the harvesting, Mike decided to give them a hand. Normally they tried not to work on the weekend, but it was necessary to harvest a field of strawberries, as they were just right for picking and taking to market. In order to preserve their freshness, they had to be picked now and transported. They worked in the hot sun until noon, but still were not finished.

Mike went to the house for lunch. Thinking about Reba, he was hoping he could keep his mind occupied by staying busy with his work.

"Your lunch is on the table Mike," Sally told him, as he entered the house. "Thanks, Sally."

Mike washed his hands in the downstairs bathroom and entered the dining room.

"Hi, Mike. Come in; it is just the two of us for lunch.

The ladies and Johnny have gone into town shopping," Mr. Davis informed him.

"Oh, that's nice; how are you, sir?"

"Fine, Mike, How are they doing with the strawberries?" Mr. Davis asked.

"Coming along good. I think we'll have them out by this afternoon. It will take all afternoon, though."

"Yes, a very good crop this time around. The rain came just at the right time."

Mike and Mr. Davis continued chatting as they ate their lunch. Soon it was time to go back to work and continue harvesting the strawberries. About 3:00 P.M. Mike had a phone call and went to his room to take it.

"Hello?" said Mike, expectantly.

"Hello, is this Mike?" It was a man's voice. "Yes, this is Mike; who is this?"

"Mike, this is Detective Lewis Hawkins of the Los Angeles Police Department. I'm the person you talked with when you reported the box that you found buried."

"Yes, I remember now. What can I do for you?"

"Mike, I was wondering if you could come down and talk to me on Monday at the station?"

"Yes, I could do that, ifyou think it would help."

"Well, it might help, and we sure would appreciate it," he said.

"What time would be best?" Mike asked.

"Nine or ten o'clock Monday morning would be fine, anytime around there, I will be there all morning," he said.

"Okay then, I'll be down there at that time," said Mike.

"Right, see you then, and thanks, Mike," the detective said.

"No problem. Goodbye," Mike said, as they hung up their phones.

Mike went back to the field thinking about the call.

"I hope Donald doesn't get into trouble over this; he might already be in trouble, though. Nobody has seen him lately; wonder where he is?

It's got to be hard on Johnny and Valerie. Johnny is such a nice kid, and she is such a nice lady."

Mike and the other workers finished the job of getting the strawberries harvested, and the last truck was on the way to market. It was an hour past dinnertime when Mike was going up to his room. Mr. and Mrs. Davis were on the front lawn.

"Hi, Mike, I am heating up your dinner. It will be on the table; Sally has gone home." Mike recognized Valerie's voice.

"Oh, okay, thanks; how you doing?" he said, while going further up the steps.

"Fine, Mike," Valerie said.

"I'll be right down as soon as I wash up." He went on to his room.

Mike returned and went into the dining room. His plate was in what had become his usual place. Right across from him was Valerie. She had a glass of wine in front of her and had poured Mike one.

She was wearing a red low-cut blouse, which was revealing just enough, along with a loose fitting black skirt. She looked beautiful.

She picked up her glass and held it up to Mike. "Here is to you, Mike," she said.

"Here is to you, Valerie," he said, raising his glass. "Thanks for the dinner. We got the job done, but it took a little longer than we thought it would," he said.

"Mike, you are a hard worker. You didn't have to work today, and you put a full day in yesterday," she said, with a concerned look on her face.

"As long as I am busy, I don't have time to think," he said.

"You mean about Reba?"

"Reba and other things, Valerie," he said.

"How did it go last night, when you talked to her?"

"She left for Vegas with the guy last night. It's all over between us," he said.

"I'm sorry, Mike; I know it isn't easy for you," she said, looking concerned.

"How did the shopping go today?" he said, changing the subject.

"Oh, it was fun; we picked up a few bargains with the sales that were on. I got a new bathing suit and a few other things. Found a nice little suit for Johnny that fits him perfectly; he looks good in it," she said.

"I'll bet you look good in your suit, too," he said.

"It did fit me good, but there isn't much to it," she blushed.

"Oh, it must be a bikini?"

"Yes, it is. And it was on sale; a good buy," she said. Mike continued his meal, and Mr. and Mrs. Davis and Johnny came in from outside. Mr. and Mrs. Davis spoke and went down the hall to their room. Johnny came in, sitting by his mother.

"Mom, can I watch TV awhile?" Johnny asked his mother. "Hi, Mike," he added.

"Yes, you can watch a little while, and then it will be time for your bath," she said.

"Hi, Johnny, how are you doing, big man," Mike asked.

"Doing fine; see you later," Johnny said, as he left to watch TV.

"Thanks, Valerie, that was good," Mike said, pushing his plate away from him.

"Care for some more?" she asked.

"No, No thanks, it was very good, though; I am full."

"Want to take a walk out back?" Mike asked, standing and putting his chair under the table.

"I'd love to. You go ahead, and I'll just put these dishes away and catch up to you," she said, carrying his plate and glass to the kitchen.

Mike went up to his room and removed one of the bottles of bourbon from the bag. Leaving the other bottle of bourbon still in the bag, he took the one he removed downstairs. He passed the kitchen door and looked in and saw Valerie washing his plate.

"Do you like bourbon and ginger?" he asked.

"Yes I do," she said.

"I've got the bourbon, if you bring the ginger," he said.

"Okay, and I'll bring glasses too," she smiled anticipatorily.

Mike walked on outside and went through the back gate.

He cracked open the bottle and took a good pull, straight from the bottle. He stopped outside the gate and waited for Valerie to come outside. Walking over to a bench, he sat down.

In a couple of minutes, Valerie came through the gate and looked around until she spotted Mike. She had two glasses and a bottle of ginger ale with her. She set them on the little oblong table of stone, in front of the bench. Mike was seated at one end of the bench, and she sat down beside him in the middle.

"Looks like you started without me, but you deserved it," she said, smiling at him.

"Let me fix us a drink," he said, and set about to do so.

Mike mixed each of them a drink and handed Valerie hers.

"Here is to us," they both said at the same time, as they held up their glasses. They laughed and took a sip.

It was another beautiful night. The sky was ablaze with red and orange colors changing in intensity as the sun was slowly being swallowed by the horizon. They sat quietly and watched the sunset while looking out over the fields and enjoying the beauty that surrounded them. They sat there and finished their drink.

"Care for another?" asked Mike.

"Yes, thank you, Mr. Bartender," she kidded him. "Coming right up." Mike fixed another one for them. "Mike, you make a toast this time," she said, holding her glass up as she waited for the toast.

Mike held up his glass and looked at her.

"Here is to Valerie and Mike, and the future," he said.

"Oh, I like that toast; I will drink to that," she said, as she looked at Mike while taking a sip.

They communicated to each other with their eyes locked together as they slowly raised their glasses and took another sip. Remaining in the same position, they took another sip. After the third sip, they both lowered their glasses, and their eyes magnetically drew their heads closer together. Very softly and gently their lips became joined and remained there for a minute. The restraints that had kept them from doing that before now, had been released. Valerie was breathing heavily and had to withdraw in order to catch her breath. Both their hearts were pounding as if they wanted to pound right out of their chests.

"Mike, that was so sweet," she gushed, "I haven't been kissed in such a long time, I have to catch my breath." She took another sip of her drink as Mike did, still looking at each other.

"It was wonderful, Valerie," Mike said, as he reached for her.

She responded and moved closer to him.

"Mike, kiss me again, and then I have to go put Johnny to bed; but I will be back," she said, in a very eager voice with much excitement.

"Do you promise to come back?" he teased her.

"Oh yes, I promise," she said, smiling.

Their lips once again found each other and pressed together very softly and gently, then a little harder, until Valerie had to withdraw for a breath again.

"Mike, oh Mike, you just take my breath away and I have to come up for air," she said, as she held onto him tightly and kissed him gently on the neck. Mike could feel her breasts against his chest, and he was getting excited.

"Valerie, you feel so good, I don't want to let you go," Mike confessed, as he hugged her into his chest.

"I don't want to go either, but I must put Johnny to bed now," she said, while grabbing Mike's head with both hands, and pulling his willing lips to hers, into another embrace accompanied with heavy breathing, until once again it was broken with a gasp and the sound of a deep breath.

"I will be right back," she said, standing up and reaching for her drink. She took the last of it, which wasn't much, in one gulp and handed the glass to Mike.

"May I have another, please?" she asked as she walked to the gate.

"It will be waiting for you, and so will I," he smiled at her.

"Good, I'll be right back," she said, and she went through the gate.

After finishing his drink, Mike made them both another and set them on the bench in front of him.

His thoughts remained on Valerie and the present as he relived the preceding moments with her. *She is so beautiful and she felt so good against me, her lips tasted great. It makes me hungry for more, much more. I want her.* He was still fantasizing when she came back through the gate with a shawl, which was much like a blanket, wrapped around her.

"You aren't cold, are you?" he said, as he retrieved her drink and handed it to her when she was in front of him.

"No, I brought this in case it cooled off, as it often does after the sun goes down," she said, raising her glass to him for another toast. This time she made the toast.

"Here is to the present time, and these wonderful moments together," she said.

"Yes, I agree," he said, and they drank. "Want to take that walk?" asked Mike.

"Yes, lead the way," she picked up the bottle of ginger ale and put the cap on it.

He did likewise with the bourbon.

They kissed briefly, as best they could with both had full hands; but it was not enough, as they pushed into each other. Their hearts were pounding, and Valerie had to break off to get some air; so they started strolling down toward the fields of vegetables.

They were like two dry sponges that had fallen into a bucket of water and soaking it up, but they were a long way from being saturated.

They continued to walk, frequently stopping to take a sip of their drink and taste each other's lips again, with the same results each time. Their hearts would pound in their chests and both would come up panting for air. The two sponges continued to soak up the water, but were not nearly saturated.

They passed the field where Mike had worked all day. Off in the distance, about twice as far as they had walked, they could see the hazy glow of the lights shining from the quarters where the workers lived. The fog was moving in over the valley quickly, and would soon reach them.

"Look at the lights in the fog, isn't it beautiful?" said Valerie.

"It sure is, and you are beautiful," said Mike, as he met her lips with his in another of the continuing embraces, absent of the benefit of their arms. Their arms added only minimal assistance as they were both filled with their drinks; but they did very well, coming up for a breath of air as they continued to walk.

Having passed the strawberry field, they came upon a cornfield and the corn was high. It would need to be harvested the next week.

"Let's go in there," Mike said, steering Valerie into the cornfield.

CHAPTER

12

They went deep into the cornfield. Stopping in the middle of the cornfield, Mike set his drink and the bottle down and began tramping down the corn in about an eight-foot circle. When he had finished, he took the shawl from around her shoulders and spread it out on the foot-high pile of the stalks of corn.

The stalks of corn were now lying flat, providing a comfortable place to sit down or lie down.

Mike and Valerie placed their drinks and bottles beside the pile of corn stalks and sat down beside of each other on the heap. Their previously restrained arms took full advantage of their welcomed freedom, and they embraced eagerly.

Their lips quickly met, resulting in a very intense and passionate kiss, as they fell backward on the pile of corn stalks. It was as if the dry sponge had gone into overtime in soaking the water from the bucket. The exploring hands of each of them worked feverishly, searching to find skin, groping at their cumbersome clothes. Frantically, they searched for the hidden treasures, covered by their clothes, as they continued to taste the sweetness of their kisses over and over. Finally, with the clothes discarded, Valerie gasped loudly with abandonment as Mike found her. Locked together, rocking on the corn for a long time, Valerie and Mike shared their pent-up passions, having reached a state of ecstasy. Over and over, the waves of passion found them as Valerie's nails dug into Mike's back. She groaned joyously as each wave of passion lifted her higher and higher to a point of ecstatic joy, which was unfamiliar to her, never having reached such heights before or so many times. Both sweating profusely, they continued to rock back and forth, not wanting the moment to end. Suddenly, after a long time, and having reached the peak several times with minor explosions, they once again reached the highest peak, and went over the top. This time it was as if a volcano had erupted, and they exploded together. Over and over, again in waves of violent convulsiveness, the sudden release of their pent-up feelings and emotions filled them with immeasurable joy. The intense rocking became slower as they continued to exchange kisses softly, and then harder. Not wanting their state of supreme fulfillment to end, they rocked lovingly, still completely entwined and locked together. The fog had moved over the valley and hung through the cornfield like a canopy. The moon had now changed positions in the sky.

"Oh, Mike, oh, Mike," she cried, as he bore down on her, taking her back closer to the top of the peak again. "Oh, Mike, it is wonderful," she said, "It is wonderful," she gasped, and held on as she approached the top.

"Oh! Yes! Yes! Mike!" she said loudly, her eyes rolling, as she entered into a state of delirium. She was delectably filled with love when he exploded again and again, simultaneously, with her. They had just experienced, together, all of the joy of the ultimate consummation.

Remaining there quietly, until finally Mike rolled over on his side, she faced him and snuggled up close to him.

"Oh, Mike, that was wonderful; so beautiful!" she whispered, as they caressed.

"Fantastic! You are great!" he said, as his normal breathing returned slowly.

"You are so beautiful, Valerie, such a beautiful lover."

"Oh, Mike, sweet precious Mike," she kissed him tenderly.

The fog increased as they continued to whisper endearments, while exchanging tender kisses. The moon penetrated the fog just enough for Mike to see her face.

All of their fantasies had been fulfilled; all of their questions had been answered, at least as far as their love making was concerned.

Their pulse-rate and breathing slowly descended as they rested together on the pile of corn stalks. Facing each other, they kissed tenderly as they stroked each other lovingly.

After quite some time, they stirred and sat up.

Mike put his arms back around Valerie and pulled her gently, yet tightly, into him and kissed her hard.

"You are wonderful, Valerie, so precious." he said

"Oh, Mike, it is wonderful being with you," she whispered, as she kissed him again.

They began to put their clothes on and get themselves composed. After checking around, as best they could, to be sure they had everything, they walked out of the cornfield and back the way they had come, toward the house.

"I wish we could sleep together tonight," Mike said.

"I do, too, Mike, but with Mom, Dad and Johnny there, I guess we had better not," her mind said to concede, but her heart said something entirely different.

As they walked up through the heavy fog, the dim lights of the house could barely be seen. Their bodies could be seen only from the waist up as they reluctantly walked to the house where they would separate for the night.

"Mike, I can't bare the thought of not being with you tonight," she confessed, yearning for a solution. She didn't want to disrupt the household, and yet the magnetic pull of her feelings for Mike were overpowering.

"I want you in my arms tonight, Valerie; I don't want to be alone without you." The thought of them not being together now, after what they had just experienced, was painful.

"And you shall have me in your arms, and I shall have you in mine," she said, yielding to the overpowering desire of her heart.

They stopped walking and faced each other, putting the bottles and glasses on the ground, and embraced as they lovingly kissed, celebrating their decision that no matter what, it was too much to ask to be separated tonight. They could not accept that. Their love was so strong that they were willing to face whatever came in the aftermath, come hell or high water, they would be together tonight.

They resumed their walk through the fog and found the back gate.

"Mike, I am going to shower, and I'll be over to your room," she whispered, as they approached the back door.

"I'll be waiting," he said.

Valerie put the ginger ale in the refrigerator and the glasses in the sink as Mike silently went to his room and the shower.

On the way to her room, Valerie looked in on Johnny and found him sleeping soundly. She proceeded to her room and the shower.

Later on, Mike lay in bed anticipating Valerie's return to his arms. He became mesmerized when he heard the faint wail of a train's whistle off in the distance. He returned in his mind to the days of his youth when he lay in his bed and heard the whistle and the clatter of the steel wheels rolling by outside of his window. He had answered the whistle's call, and had ridden on destiny's train. The train had carried him to a new life of abundance and into the arms of the girl of his dreams.

The small lamp on the dresser gave a soft glow to the room. Soon Valerie entered and, very quietly, she placed a bottle of brandy and two glasses on the table by the door. She then closed the door and locked it. Mike leaned back on his pillow with his hands behind his head and enjoyed the view.

She poured them a brandy and went over to Mike, handing him his drink. She had on a red negligee, and she looked gorgeous. She had applied a light coat of red lipstick that matched the color of the negligee. Her beautiful long dark hair fell down loosely and framed her just-scrubbed face. The just-completed lovemaking session in the cornfield had left her with an afterglow that remained with her, lighting up her face and causing her eyes to sparkle. They said nothing and raised their glasses in a pointing gesture and then sipped the brandy. Mike feasted his eyes, but could not stand it any longer. He sat his glass down on the table by the bed. Taking his lead, Valerie did the same. She turned the light off and slipped down beside him, snuggling up in his arms. They kissed tenderly and repeatedly, gently stroking each other. They knew that they had made the right decision to be together. Quietly and thoroughly, they shared and discovered their bodies as they continued throughout the night to drift together in the sea of love. Over and over again, they reached the peak of ecstasy, carefully stifling their desire to loudly verbalize the joy they felt, choosing to suffice in its place, whispered words of endearment. After briefly falling into dreamland for a nap, one of them would move and the gentle love feast would once again be aroused. Then they would sweetly kiss until desire built within them. Their rhythmic rocking soon catapulted them on yet another trip to the peak of ecstasy, to the point where they exploded in waves of joy.

"Oh, Mike!" she whispered. "Valerie, my precious."

Outside, the fog rolled throughout the valley.

Inside, Mike and Valerie experienced love like they had never known it before.

They continued throughout the night to tenderly express their love. They wished for the night to never end.

Their appetite for each other was insatiable. They continued as long as they possibly could, but sometime in the wee hours, filled with the joy of their newly found love, they floated off to dreamland on a soft cloud.

Lightning cracked loudly and struck a tree, about twenty feet past the back gate, and Valerie and Mike both woke up. Then the rain came down hard. Valerie slipped out of bed and went over and closed the window, then returned to Mike.

"I have to go check Johnny," she said, in a low voice.

She gave him a quick kiss and was gone, putting the sheer robe on as she left, carrying her negligee and bikini panties in her hand. She went to her room, got her silk robe and went to Johnny's room. He was awake and sitting up in bed, looking straight ahead with the blanket pulled up to his chin.

"Hi, sweetheart, that was a loud one, wasn't it?" She comforted him as she hugged him to her.

"Will you stay with me a while, Mom?" he asked. "Sure sweetheart, just let me go to the bathroom and I'll be right back," she said.

"Okay, I have to go, too, so I'll be right here when you come back," he said.

"Okay, sweetheart, I'll be right back."

Johnny went to his bathroom, and Valerie went to hers.

Afterwards, she looked in the mirror and frowned.

"My hair is a mess, but it was sure worth it, " she said, going back to Johnny's room.

She and Johnny were soon asleep, as was Mike.

Later on, about 9:00A.M., Valerie and Johnny woke up and showered and got dressed. Johnny was in his new suit, and Valerie had on her nice blue suit. She had fixed her hair and was all made up and looked beautiful. They went downstairs and joined Mr. and Mrs. Davis, who also were dressed up nice. They all had a nice breakfast together, which Sally had prepared.

After breakfast, they were off to Sunday school and church.

Mike came down shortly after they left and had breakfast. Having had a rough week, he enjoyed sleeping late. The rain had stopped. The sun, which was now out brightly, would quickly dry things off.

He was thinking about his appointment tomorrow with the detective. *"I don't know what I can do to help them. They still haven 't found Donald apparently. It is too bad for Johnny and for Valerie,*

*although Valerie is another matter now. I miss her already, and she just
left my bed a few hours ago.*

Mike had fallen for Valerie and was falling more every time he
thought of her.

About 12:30 P.M., everybody came home from church.

Mike was in the back, looking at the tree that had been struck
by lightning. After they had changed clothes, Johnny and Valerie
came out and joined Mike.

"Hi, Mike," said Johnny.

"Hi, Johnny, look at where the lightning hit the tree," Mike
pointed.

"Hello, Mike, how are you doing?" Valerie grinned.

"I'm doing great Valerie; how about you."

"I'm doing wonderfully well, thanks." She puckered a kiss to
him that Johnny didn't see.

"Mom, can I go play with Carlos?" Johnny asked.

"Yes, okay, son," she answered.

Carlos was Johnny's closest friend around there. He was a little
older, and they were great pals. Johnny went running over to the
house where Carlos lived, and in a little while they were running
down toward the fields throwing a football. Mike and Valerie were
alone outside, and the Davises were in the house. Sally had Sunday
afternoons off, so she had gone home. Mr. and Mrs. Davis were
going into town later, and they mentioned taking Johnny with
them, but didn't say what time they would leave. Mike and Valerie
walked back from the tree to the bench where they had sat last
night. The shrubs along the back fence offered the only measure of
privacy around, since the bench was hidden and out of sight from
the Valetta's house.

"Hi, Mike, I have missed you so much today. Man! It was
wonderful last night," she gushed, when they were alone on the
bench.

"Oh, Valerie, I have yearned for you today. Yes, it was fantastic;
I want you so much right now I can hardly stand it," he said.

"I have an appointment tomorrow in town, can you go with me, by any chance? After the appointment, we could spend the whole day together," he said.

Mike and Carlos were now out of sight over the little hill that went down to the fields. They seized the opportunity.

Valerie moved over by Mike and embraced him as her lips found his. They found a little comfort for the pain of separation they had endured in the previous few hours. They were still extremely hungry for each other. The entire night of love had only increased their desire for each other. Mike felt her breasts rubbing against his pounding chest as she began to breathe deeply with the rush of fiery passion surging through her, which had been kindled by their relentless kisses. She finally broke away, coming up for air, and answered him.

"Oh, baby, I can't think right now," she gushed, "but I will think about it later and try to think of some way that we can make it work. It would be wonderful to be with you for part of the day at least. Mike I am falling hard for you," she confessed, with a sincere look on her face.

"I can't seem to get enough of you, Valerie. You are really becoming an obsession to me. I don't like being away from you, and I know there are times when I must," Mike said, reaching for her, wrapping his strong arms around her. He gripped her into his pounding chest like a vice, kissing her hard and hungrily.

"Mike, oh, Mike." she gasped, "lets slow down a little; I can't take it; you have me wanting to climb the walls, and I need to catch my breath. Man! I want you right now," she said.

Just then Johnny and Carlos came running up toward them.

"Mom, guess what, the aliens have been here!" he said excitedly.

"Yes, we saw where they had been, you wouldn't believe what we saw," Carlos chimed in.

"The aliens have been here, Mom, and they were right down there in the cornfield!" he asserted.

"What are you talking about Johnny?" she asked.

"The aliens have been here and made one of those patterns like we saw on TV that time, remember? You and Mike come and see," he urged them.

Mike and Valerie followed the two boys down to the cornfield, and Johnny led them to where they had made love the night before.

Mike and Valerie smiled at each other.

"Looks like they were here all right," said Mike.

"I'll bet they had a good time playing around in our cornfield," said Valerie, as she looked up and smiled at Mike.

"This is my first time seeing where an alien has been," Johnny said.

"Mine too, but we'll have to be on the look out for the aliens now," said Carlos.

"Come on, Carlos, lets go look for some aliens," said Johnny.

Carlos and Johnny ran out of the cornfield.

Mike went over and sat on the pile of corn stalks.

Valerie went over and sat down beside of him with a sheepish grin on her face.

"So, that is what you are, an alien huh?" she said, and laughed.

"You sure put me into outer space, baby," they laughed again.

"I love rocketing off to the moon with you," Mike said.

They kissed and rolled back onto the pile as they had done the previous night. Lying there, embraced as they were, they felt the love emanating back and forth between them. They could have stayed there another night, but had to exercise restraint now. After another embrace filled with kisses, they got up and left the corn- field.

They went back up to the house for the evening meal. Carlos was just going home, and Johnny went into the house with them. They had a light meal of sandwiches and potato salad that Sally had made earlier for them.

After the meal, Mr. and Mrs. Davis took Johnny and went into town to see some friends. They planned to stop, on their way home, to talk with a man who was a business associate of Mr. Davis. They said they would be home about 10:30 P.M.

As they went down the road, Valerie turned to Mike. "How about a drink, darling?" she asked.

"Yes, I would love one," he said. "Do you want brandy?"

"Yes, brandy would be fine," said Mike.

Valerie began to fix the drinks, and Mike went into the den and sat on the sofa. She soon returned and handed Mike his drink. She sat down beside Mike with her drink. Mike had the drink in his left hand, and reached over and put his right arm around Valerie.

"To us," he said, and they sipped, and then he pulled her over and they kissed passionately.

"It sure has been a wonderful couple of days, Valerie."

"Oh, I know, it has been wonderful, Mike, just wonderful," she leaned closer to him.

"What are we going to do, Mike, I just want to be with you so much. They are bound to get on to us sooner or later."

"I hope the aliens don't tell them," Mike said, laughing.

"Oh Mike, ifI am dreaming, please don't wake me."

"You are fantastic, sweetheart," he said, looking at her and tightening his arm around her.

"Mike, I was thinking, I could drive my car tomorrow and meet you down in the city," she said.

He kissed her hard, and once again she lost her breath.

CHAPTER 13

Mike and Valerie remained on the sofa for quite some time, enjoying the relief of the unrestricted feelings of freedom. It was refreshing to not worry if they would be seen. Taking full advantage of the time they had, they enjoyed each other to the fullest.

"Mike, oh, Mike, tell me this is real, and I am not dreaming," she said.

"Valerie, I am falling in love with you. It is a little scary, being so fast and all, but I am falling, nonetheless," he said.

"Mike, I know that I love you. I just don't want to be somebody that you are having a fling with on the rebound from losing Reba," she said.

"Are you sure about this, Mike?"

"That's funny; you mentioned Reba, and I haven't thought about her lately."

"I cared about Reba, and I think I loved her, but when she told me she had met someone else and was going to Vegas with him, something happened inside me," he said, trying to articulate his feelings.

"At first I was really hurt. I was shocked and felt very isolated. I didn't know where to turn; but then I found you. I don't know about rebound; but I do know that I felt something for you the first time I saw you. I still care about Reba, but now it's more like caring for a friend. I told her I would always love her, and be there for her if she needed me; but the love I had for her is different. I do love her as a person, and I think she is really a good person, but I feel she is being led down a path. I think the man she met is taking advantage of her gullibility."

"Who is the man, Mike?"

"He is a director that she met and got a small part in his movie," he explained.

"What is his name?"

"Joseph Maxwell, I believe it is."

"I have heard of him and, guess what, Mike?" she said.

"What?"

"He is married."

"What! Do you mean to tell me that Reba took off with a married man?" He was shocked.

"He sure is married, and not to his first wife either.

He has been married either two or three times, I forgot which," she said.

"Oh, my goodness, poor Reba, getting herself mixed up with a guy like that. I was afraid of that. She is so good-looking and gullible. I hope she is all right and gets away from him. He will only use her to his advantage."

"Yes, unfortunately, that is true and, when he is finished with her, he will discard her like garbage. It happens so much out here, Mike," she said, folding her hands and looking down at them.

"There isn't much I can do to help her, but I wish there was," he said apathetically.

"Well, she knows how to get in touch with you, if she needs you, Mike." She patted his hand.

"I support you in your decision to remain her friend and be there for her if she needs you, Mike; I think it is admirable of you to offer her that."

"Well, after all, we did come out here together, and neither of us knew anyone out here, so I feel some responsibility for her."

"But you are my love interest now and, rebound, or whatever it is, I do love you; I want you."

"Oh, Mike, my darling, Mike, I love you too."

Her lips found his, and they embraced until she came up for air, then stood up and pulled his hand so that he stood. She led him to the stairs. They went into Mike's room, where they had spent the previous night, and each started peeling off their clothes. They locked the door and, lying down on the bed, they began kissing each other wildly with passion. In a few minutes, he found her, and she verbalized her willingness in a loud voice without constraint. They began their ride again, back to the top of the mountain, which they had reached so many times recently.

The next couple of hours were spent further cementing their love as they experienced joyous thrills of passion, so intense, that neither had previously known of their existence. The stratospheric heights to which they soared were not only previously unknown to them, but their ability to reach those heights so many times, and still remain hungry for them, was amazing.

Not only did this ability speak of the addictiveness of this passion, but said to them that they had discovered a very rare treasure, when they had found each other, and experienced their love. This knowledge served to bond them together very strongly.

Not only physically, but they were becoming one in every way. With each rise to the top of the mountain, and with each endearing word or look, they became more bonded together.

After a short nap, they roused and lovingly embraced.

"I guess we had better get up before they get home, Mike, but I sure don't want to," she said.

"I suppose so, if we don't want to be discovered." Reluctantly, they got up, and Valerie kissed Mike and went to her room. Mike took a quick shower and got dressed.

It had been nice to be there alone, and enjoy being together freely, without the pressure of having others around and worrying about getting caught. They hoped to find a solution soon, and could be open about their love. Right now, there was too much going on for them to try thinking about working it out. All they could do was to be together as much as they could, and however they could. Whether in the cornfield, or alone at night, when everyone was asleep.

"Oh no, they will harvest the corn this week and cut the cornfield down. The poor aliens worked so hard building that design, and now it will be destroyed. What will the aliens do now, and where will they go to make love?" Hmm

"I'll bet they come up with some good idea that will get them together" Mike mused, as he exited his room with a big smile on his face.

Valerie spotted his big grin, as she was just about to go down the stairs.

"What is that big grin all about?" she said, smiling and waiting for him to reach her.

"I was just wondering where the aliens were going to go next week when they harvest the corn and cut all the stalks down?"

"I'll bet *they* think of something, won't *we,*" she said, as they both laughed happily while descending the stairs.

It was just about 10:30 P.M. when the Davises and Johnny got home. Since it was so late, after a short visit, the Davis's said goodnight and went to their room.

Valerie went up and tucked Johnny in for the night, and Mike went to his room. It would be another eventful day tomorrow and everybody was tired.

Mike undressed and lay on his bed alone thinking of Valerie. She had really blown him away, and he was obsessed with her. He knew that he was experiencing a very deep love that he had not felt with Reba. He had loved Reba, but it was not the same. He was very concerned for Reba, and he hoped he did hear from her, and that she would be all right.

Mike lay on the bed and mused about the events of the past few days. Many things had happened in such a short time. *"I think I have run the gamut of emotions, from the depths of depression, to the ultimate high, this weekend. I was thrown into a tailspin by Reba on Friday, and fell hopelessly in love with Valerie shortly thereafter. The remainder of the weekend has shown me that I have found the woman of my dreams and the love of my life."*

Just then Mike heard the doorknob tum, and Valerie came into the room. She silently closed and locked the door.

She had worn her beautiful silk robe and removed it quickly. In seconds she was snuggled in bed beside Mike, wearing only a big smile.

"Oh, how nice to have you here in my arms again," Mike said.

"I couldn't stay away; I just hope they don't catch us," she said.

"What would you tell them if they did?"

"I would tell them that I loved you deeply," she whispered.

"And I would tell them the same, and that we could not stand to be apart," he said.

"They will know anyway shortly, won't they Mike?"

"Yes, I expect they will start suspecting something before long, or we'll goof up and kiss in front of them, or something." Mike said, as they both grinned happily.

"Mike, can you meet me tomorrow at noon at Jack's Place?"

"Do you want to make it about eleven in the morning? I should be finished with my meeting in plenty of time to get there by then," he said, wanting to spend as much time with her as possible.

"That's fine; I'll meet you at eleven o'clock."

"Great, we'll go to the beach if it is nice and doesn't rain."

"Bite your tongue, Mike. No raining on our parade when I have a new bikini to wear and a chance to be with you, my sweet precious, Mike," she kissed him tenderly.

"I love you Valerie, my precious," said Mike, as he snuggled her even closer and kissed her tenderly.

"Mike, oh, Mike, I love you, too, my darling," she said.

They lay intertwined together with feelings of love so intense for each other that tears of joy began to fall softly on Mike's chest. Shortly, she felt the dampness of other tears leaking silently on her forehead, and she smiled and kissed his chest, as they both fell into a peaceful sleep.

Monday morning came and Valerie woke up and scurried quickly back to her room. On her way, she caught a glimpse of the back of her father-in-law as he just walked into the dining room. *"Whew! !just made it,"* she thought, going into her room.

Mike stirred and looked at the clock. It was 7:00A.M.

"I had better get moving, I want to get there at nine thirty this morning to see the detective. I wonder if he has any news about Donald. " Mike went to the shower.

By the time Valerie came down, Mike was eating breakfast with the Davises in the dining room. Sally was having coffee with them. She rose when Valerie entered the room, and went to the kitchen to fix her breakfast.

"Good morning, everybody," she said.

They all spoke to her and continued eating. Johnny was sleeping soundly, so Valerie left him alone. She sat down by Mike, who was in his usual place, next to Mr. Davis. Mrs. Davis was on the other side of Mr. Davis, across from Mike. After delivering Valerie her plate filled with bacon and eggs and toast, Sally took her place at the opposite end of the table.

"Thanks, Sally, this looks good." She was hungry, and began to eat immediately.

"Gloria and I are going shopping today, Mom," she lied, as she took another bite of food.

"Well, that's nice, say hello to her for me; such a sweet girl," Mrs. Davis said.

"Yes, I will, Mom, I'll be gone most of the day as we are also going to lunch. We might go to the beach for a while after lunch. We haven't been there for a while," she said.

"You need a day out with your friends now and then, Valerie, so I am glad you are going," Mrs. Davis said, looking at Valerie.

"Now don't worry about Johnny, he will be fine here. He said he wanted to watch them harvest the corn today anyway. He said that he and Carlos had seen where the aliens had been in the corn, and they want to watch them fly away when the combines go through and stir them up. Oh, he told us all about the aliens last night on the way home. What an imagination he has."

"He sure does, Mom, and thanks for looking after him. I love you for it," Valerie said, as she bumped Mike's knee under the table.

"Oh sure, it's a pleasure, and you know I'd do anything for you and Johnny," she said.

"I know, Mom, and I don't know what I would have done without you and Dad, especially lately with all that has been taking place with Donald and all." Valerie's demeanor changed, and she had a far-off look on her face.

Mr. Davis was cognizant of the change in her demeanor.

"We love you and Johnny, Val; this is your home, and it has been so nice getting to see our grandson grow up. You have given us more, really, than we have to you, and brought such fun to our household," Mr. Davis said, wanting to be supportive, having seen the way his son had treated her and Johnny.

They finished their breakfast and began leaving the dining room to get on with their day.

"Mike, you have your meeting this morning, so Jose will see that the corn gets to market, and I will be around here today, so I'll look in on them," said Mr. Davis.

"Yes sir, and I might be gone most of the day. I need to go by and see Jack and see what kind of a schedule he has for me this week.

Business has picked up, and he might need me more than usual," Mike told him, and was glad he didn't have to lie to him.

Valerie had gotten Johnny up, and he came running over to the upstairs' banister and, with both hands on the rail, he looked down at everybody.

"Hi, everybody, they have started cutting the corn already, and I've got to hurry up and get out there and see those aliens! I heard the combines running!" Johnny said enthusiastically.

"Well, get dressed Johnny, and your breakfast will be on the table. After you eat, we'll go see if we can see them," said his grandfather, smiling at Johnny.

"Mr. Davis, could we have a word in the den?" Mike asked.

"Of course," he answered, moving his hand in a sweeping motion toward the den.

Alone in the den, Mike looked at him.

"I was wondering, sir, have you heard any more from Donald?"

"Yes, I had one more call from him early last week, Monday, I believe it was; but nothing since then," said Mr. Davis.

"I think he was calling from Vegas, and he asked for twenty-thousand dollars again, but I just couldn't give it to him. I have given him money all along, five-thousand here and five-thousand there, time after time, and I have just reached the point where I just can't continue to give him money to throw away," Mr. Davis went on.

"I understand, sir." Mike thought very highly of this man, who had become a wonderful friend, and he hated to see the anguish in his face.

"I am very concerned about Donald; I don't know what he is mixed up in, or who he is with. I do know how he has been to his beautiful wife and son. He has not done right by them, and he has become a stranger to me and his mother, who also is very worried about him," he continued unburdening himself.

"Yes sir, I was just wondering if you had heard any more about him. Who knows, maybe he will be all right," Mike said, unbelieving his own words, but lacking anything else at the moment to say that might encourage Mr. Davis, which he wanted to do.

"I hope so, but frankly, I have my doubts about it."

Mr. Davis was a wise man.

"Well, good to chat with you, and we'll chat again after I talk to the detective," Mike said, heading for the door.

"You bet, Mike, anytime, and have a nice day," Mr. Davis said.

"Yes sir, you too," Mike said, as he went upstairs. "I've finished my breakfast, Granddad. Are you ready?" asked Johnny standing in the dining room doorway.

"Okay, big boy, lets go, I'm ready to see those aliens," Mr. Davis said, as they went out the back door.

Mike brushed his teeth, and was getting ready to go, when Valerie silently came in the door with a big smile on her face. He walked over to her with opened arms, which she soon filled. They kissed, lovingly.

"I had to see you, Gloria, before you left," she said, with a big grin on her face.

"I wanted to see you too, you little fibber," he said.

"I had to come up with something, and I thought it was rather clever," she smiled.

"It seems to have been, darling; Golly, I love you," he said, as he kissed her passionately.

"Whoa! I love you too, but don't get me going now, we don't have time," she said, gasping for air.

"I know, in fact I have to be going," he said.

"Okay, sweetheart, I'll see you at Jack's Place later," she said, kissing him quickly, as she left the room.

Mike waited a few minutes and then went downstairs and out the front door. Valerie would leave a little later.

The sun was shining brightly, and it looked like a perfect day for the beach. Mike drove toward the city, anticipating the meeting.

"Maybe Detective Hawkins will have some news about Donald. I know it would relieve the family's minds if he did. It has been hard on

all of them. Mr. and Mrs. Davis have really been good to Valerie and Johnny. Thank goodness for them. They have plenty of money and can give them everything they need. Valerie has been through a lot with Donald. Man, I miss her already, and I just saw her. I sure do love her."

Mike continued his cogitation all the way to the city. At 9:20 A.M. he pulled into the parking lot of the detective's office at the police precinct. He went in and was directed to Detective Hawkins's office. Finding the office down the hall, he knocked on the door.

"Come in," came the matter-of-fact voice.

"Detective Hawkins, Mike Clark. How are you, sir?"

"Ah, Mr. Clark, come right in, glad to see you, have a seat." His greeting appeared sincere to Mike.

"Well, have you got any news about Donald, or the case?" Mike was anxious to know, and got right to the point of their meeting.

"Yes, Mike I have. I have good news and bad news, which do you want first?" Now Mike was even more anxious to know, *"get on with it, man, "* he thought.

"What is the good news?" asked Mike, slipping up to the edge of his seat, looking Detective Hawkins in the eye, anticipatorily, as he perked up his ears, waiting for what the man had to say.

"The good news is that Donald and his partner, Larry Plott, were spotted last Tuesday in Las Vegas, so we know that they were there at that time, at least," the detective finally said.

"And what is the bad news?"

"Well, the bad news is that Larry Plott was spotted again on Wednesday, but Donald was not. Neither of them have been seen since then," the detective said.

"We have people looking all over Vegas for them, and, that is not an easy task in the midst of all those people. We don't know if they have decided to split up, or if something has happened to one or both of them, or where they are, but it will come out eventually.

I do know that the two guys that we caught with the drugs that you found, and pointed out to us, were plenty ticked-off at Donald and Larry. They are in jail awaiting trial and, with their prior convictions; they probably are facing a long time in the can this time.

They thought that Donald and Larry had set them up and had tipped off the police to where the drugs were. I personally heard them talking about how they hated a rat, and that they were dead meat.

They were talking about putting out a contract later, when they were in the holding cell. I was standing around the doorway, where they couldn't see me, and heard them planning it," the detective said, as he paused and lit a cigar, offering one to Mike.

"No thanks," Mike declined the offer, "So you think that someone is trying to kill them both?" Mike knew the answer, but wanted to be sure of what the detective was saymg.

"It looks that way, Mike, unfortunately. If we can find them first, they might have a chance," he said.

"Yes, I hope you do find them. Man, I feel bad about this," Mike said, hanging his head.

"Don't blame yourself, Mike, you did your civic duty and, just think, you might have even saved some kid from taking those drugs," he said, trying to reassure Mike that he had done the right thing. He didn't think he had succeeded.

"Of course they would have just gotten them from another supplier," he conceded.

"Mike, you must realize that by your actions, we might be able to track this thing back to the main supplier. We might catch not only the two hoodlums that we already have in jail, but several others as well." He felt better now and more successful.

"Yes, I suppose you are right about it, but Donald and that other guy; I just feel bad about that," Mike said. "Because of me, they could be shot or something, gosh, I don't know," said Mike.

"Mike," the detective was tenacious in wanting to ease Mike's mind and explaining the situation to him, "try to look at it this way," he began. "If you run around with dogs, you are subject to getting fleas. Dealing drugs is a dangerous and sometimes, in fact, I am going to say often times, a deadly business. Sometimes people get hurt, but it comes with the territory.

Don't blame yourself, Mike. If you hadn't found the drugs, something else would have happened to bring it to a head, and something maybe worse. They could have killed a bunch of innocent people. No telling what good you have done here. No, there is a price to pay, and they all pay it, sooner or later. You have done this city and country a favor by what you did. Don't feel bad about it; just be glad for taking these thugs and criminals off the streets," he paused again, and took a drag off of the stinking cigar, rolling in his mouth like it was a lollipop.

Mike listened intently to the veteran and wise detective, and he did feel better after listening to him.

"Well, I am sure you are right. You have been in this business a lot longer than I have, so I hope you do get those guys off the streets. They do ruin a lot of lives, and they will do practically anything to get their drugs," Mike said.

"No, Mike, not just practically, they will do *anything,* period."

'Thanks for all you've said. I do feel better about it. I am sorry if someone gets hurt, but there isn't anything I can do about it," Mike said as he stood up.

"Is there anything else I need to know about concerning the case?" he asked.

"No, not at this time, Mike. Stay in touch, though, and if anything significant develops, I will call you." Detective Hawkins stood up and extended his hand.

Mike shook his hand.

"Thanks a lot, Detective Hawkins, I'll be in touch," Mike said.

"Anytime, Mike, here is my card, and my home number is on there. Call day or night as you want to," he said.

Mike thanked him and took the card. He put it in his wallet on the way to his car.

It was a short drive over to Jack's Place, and Mike parked in the same spot that he had parked in the last Friday night he had worked. He got there right at 11:00A.M., and Valerie had not yet arrived. He walked into the bar.

"Hi, Mike, how you doing, man?" called Jack when he saw him.

"Hello, Jack, how is it going?" said Mike, walking over to the bar and taking a seat. "Care for a drink, buddy?"

"Yeah, and thanks. Fix me two Margaritas, will you?"

The comers of Jack's mouth turned down.

"Hmm, one for each hand, huh?" Jack said, not wanting to be nosy.

Jack made the drinks and set them in front of Mike.

"Here you are, kid. Say, are you expecting someone?" Jack said, while thinking, *what's a little nosiness among friends."*

"I sure am, Mike, I sure am," he said.

"You sure do heal fast, Mike. That booze must have drowned all those troubles you had, never did work for me, but hey, I still try every now and then," Jack said, smiling, while leaning over the bar like he didn't want anyone to know the secret.

Just then Valerie came through the door wearing a white pair of slacks and a maroon short-sleeved blouse. Her hair was all fixed up; she was made up to be gorgeous, which didn't take much make up at all. She looked beautiful, and she turned every head in the place.

Once she spotted Mike, she walked straight over and sat down on the bar stool next to him.

"Is this seat taken, sir?" she smiled at Mike.

"Now it is, by the most gorgeous girl in the world," he answered, as he leaned over and kissed her briefly.

Mike slid the Margarita over to her. "Here is to us," she said.

"You say the sweetest things," he said.

They each took a sip and then looked at Jack.

Jack was standing there with his head tilted, his brow furrowed and his mouth open, just taking it all in as if he had been struck speechless.

"My goodness son, you've been holding out on me, big time. You ain't nothing but a hound dog, that's what you are, a big ole hound dog."

They all had a good laugh.

"Valerie, this is Jack. Jack, this is Valerie"

"Well, well, well, how do you do?" said Jack.

"Fine, Jack, I am pleased to meet you, I've heard some nice things about you," she said.

"Ah, you can't believe everything you hear, you know, somebody probably starting rumors." he said.

Valerie liked him right off.

"I'll bet everything nice that I heard is true, I can just tell," she said.

"You didn't hear them from an ole hound dog, did you?" he asked, laughing. They had another good laugh.

"Are you hungry, Valerie?" Mike asked.

"Yes, I could eat a cheeseburger, sweetheart," she said. "Jack, could we get a couple of cheeseburgers, please?" Mike asked.

"You bet you can, sweetheart, you ole hound dog you," Jack said, milking it for all it was worth. He wrote the order and passed it through the window to the cook.

They laughed again, and Jack moved to the other end of the bar to wait on a customer.

"What a character, honey, but a nice guy," Valerie said.

"Oh, yes, Valerie, he is the best. He would do anything in the world for you," Mike said.

The phone rang and Jack answered it. "Jack's Place, this is Jack speaking."

"Yes he is; just a minute please."

Jack brought the phone back and handed it to Mike. Mike couldn't imagine who it was, unless it was Reba.

"Hello, this is Mike," he said.

"Mike, this is Jean Davis. I was wondering if you had seen anything of Valerie?

"Oh, yes I have, she is right here; just a minute."

"Thank you, Mike."

Mike handed the phone to Valerie. "Hello?"

"Valerie, thank goodness I have found you," Mrs. Davis said.

"Why Mom, what's wrong?"

"Well, Gloria called a little while ago and said she hadn't seen you, I got worried that something had happened. I knew that Mike was going into the city, so I thought of his job at Jack's Place, and decided

to call there and see if I could, by chance, catch him there and see if he knew where you might be. Is everything all right?" she said, sounding concerned.

"Yes, Mom, everything is fine. In fact, everything is wonderful," she said, looking at Mike and smiling.

"I am sorry, Mom, that I worried you," she said.

"I don't understand, what about Gloria?"

"Mom, I lied to you, and I am sorry that I did. I thought it was the best thing to do at the time, but I see now that it was not. I am not going to put one lie on top of another one. Mom, will you just trust me, please, and know that I am all right? When I get home this evening, you and I will sit down and have a girl-to-girl talk, okay?

"Yes, of course I will trust you. I know that you are fine now, and that relieves my mind. Is Mike ...I mean are you with Mike?

"Yes, Mom, I am with Mike."

"Oh, well, I am glad you are all right. Enjoy yourself I'll see you when you get home, and I will look forward to our gab session."

"Oh, Mom?"

"Yes, honey?"

"Dad heard me this morning when I said I was going shopping with Gloria and--" said Valerie, before being interrupted by Mrs. Davis.

"Don't worry your pretty head for one minute. I am going to call Gloria back and tell her that I was mixed up, and you were going shopping with someone else. No need to say who, and if she asks, I'll tell her I forgot. That way she won't need to call back. As for Carl, what he doesn't know won't hurt him. I'll get on now, and see you tonight.

"Mom?"

"Yes, honey?"

"Mom, I love you; you are the greatest! I'll see you tonight, and thanks," Valerie said.

"Okay, honey, and be careful. Bye now; love you, too."

Valerie handed the phone to Mike, who had been watching her all that time, hoping everything was okay.

"I heard half of that conversation, so I take it that everything is fine?" Mike said.

"No, Mike, everything is wonderful," she said, reaching over and kissing him.

"Here we are, two cheeseburgers with fries on the side," Jack said, as he set them down in front of them.

They ate their cheeseburgers, had another drink, and were ready to leave.

"Jack, what is my schedule this week?" Mike asked.

"How about the same as last week, Mike?"

"Okay, suits me. Here, take this." He held up a twenty-dollar bill to Mike. "What's that for?"

"For the drinks and burgers."

"Get out of here before I get the broom after you," he waved the back of his hand at Mike.

"Thanks, Jack, see you later."

"Okay, be careful and have fun; come back again now, Valerie," he said, adding, "bring your hound dog in anytime."

"I will, Jack, thanks, and nice meeting you."

They got in Valerie's car and Mike left his car parked by the bar. As soon as they were in the car, Mike gave her a big kiss, and they were off to the beach, only a few miles away.

Driving along, Valerie said, "How was your meeting, Mike?"

"Oh, it was okay, they don't know much yet," Mike couldn't bear to tell her everything. *I think she only knows bits and pieces, and that is enough. I intend to leave it at that. Maybe the police will find Donald and Larry Plott and put them in jail. Anyway, Valerie has started divorce proceedings, so it is a matter of time before she is free and, when she is, I want to ask her to marry me.*

"A penny for your thoughts," she said, noticing his meditation.

"I guess it is too early even to think about," he said.

"Too early to think about what, darling?"

"To think about you and me getting married," he said.

"I would marry you right now if I could, Mike," she said.

"We'll just have to wait, I guess, at least until they find Donald, or until your divorce is final," he said.

"I will still be yours, darling, married or not," she said.

"I love you, Mike, and want to spend the rest of my life with you. I know it is fast, but I don't care, I have never, at any time, been as happy as you have made me."

"And I feel just that way about you, Valerie. I love you more than I ever believed was possible," he said.

They pulled into the parking space in front of the bathhouse. They proceeded immediately to their respective dressing rooms and changed into their bathing suits.

Mike finished first, and took his clothes to the car and waited for Valerie. She arrived shortly, and they locked their clothes and her purse in the trunk of the car.

"Sweetheart, you do wonders for that nice bikini," Mike, said smiling.

"Thank you, darling, what you see is what you get," she smiled back. They walked to the beach.

"I am a very lucky man," Mike said.

The beach was sparsely populated that day, and they found a nice spot to spread the blanket out on the sand.

They ran to the water and, jumping in, began to cavort, splashing each other with water and enjoying the surf. Wading out to shoulder depth, with their hands on each other's waists, they would jump each big wave that came along, and let it pass. Mike encircled his arms around Valerie and kissed her lovingly, forgetting the wave, and they got hit, going end over end. Coming up smiling, they went right back to kissing in more shallow water where they had landed. After playing around in the water for a while, they went to the blanket and lay down. It was a perfect day for the beach. White clouds filled the blue skies overhead while they lay and surveyed them. Their fingers were linked, as they lay in the warmth of the sun, with eyes closed, listening to the crashing waves pounding the shore. They enjoyed the afternoon together, absent the presence and pressure of people around who might discover them.

Mike looked over at Valerie and felt that, indeed, he was a lucky man to have the love of this beautiful woman.

He thought about Donald and his partner who, at that moment, were in great danger, wherever they were. He had accepted the fact that he had done what he had to do in alerting the police to the drugs. He didn't see any reason to explain any more to Valerie than he already had. She had been through a lot already, and he didn't want to worry her about Donald. She had made the break from Donald and accepted things as they were with him. Donald didn't see his son much, but he was still Johnny's father.

It was a scary situation. The words of the wise and experienced detective kept coming back to him. *They will do anything for their drugs,"* he had said.

Just then Valerie opened her eyes and saw Mike looking at her.

"Are you all right, sweetheart?" she said, sensing his serious look, and perceiving that something was bothering him.

Not wanting to lie to her, and not wanting to hurt her, he told her what he could.

"I was just thinking about the meeting with the detective, and I was hoping that things would soon be worked out for everybody," he said.

"I know, I do too, sweetheart," she said.

"I love you, and I don't want to see you hurt any more, Valerie," he said.

"I know, baby, and I want things to be settled so that we can be together, too," she said.

"Oh yes, definitely," Mike said, as they shared a smile.

"We will work it out somehow, darling," she said.

"Yes we will work it out. I am so glad that I found you. I don't think I could bear to lose you," he said.

"It will work out, darling, for us; it just has to," she assured him.

"I don't ever want to lose you, either," she added.

Mike and Valerie had a great day together at the beach, going in the water a while, then lounging on the beach, and then going back into the water for a while.

That evening they slowly walked back to the bathhouse and changed into their clothes.

Going down the road, heading back to pick up Mike's car, Valerie looked over as she drove.

"It has been a great day being here with you, Mike."

"I have enjoyed every minute of it, sweetheart," she said.

They soon arrived back at Jack's Place, and Mike got out of her car.

"Want to go eat somewhere?" he asked.

"Sure baby, I am hungry, and I know you are," she answered.

"Yes, I am. How about if I let you choose the restaurant. You know them around here better than I do."

"No problem, just follow me," she said.

Mike followed Valerie's car to a place, called The Stardust, that she liked, which was not far from where they were.

They had an excellent seafood meal, and then Valerie followed Mike's car home. It was just getting dark when they pulled up in front of the house. Johnny and Mr. Davis and Mrs. Davis were in the house when they went in.

15

Johnny came running to his mother when he saw her. Mike came in shortly after she did.

"Hi, Mom," said Johnny.

"Hi, my little man, how are you?" she said, picking him up and kissing him.

"Hi, Mike," Johnny said.

"Hi there, Johnny, good to see you," Mike said, as he patted him playfully on the back.

"Mike, have you and Valerie had your dinner?" Mrs.

Davis asked, looking at Mike first, and then Valerie. "Yes, thank you; we ate at the Stardust," Mike said. "Oh, good, that is a nice place," she said.

"How was your meeting, Mike?" asked Mr. Davis. "Oh, it was fine; want to go into the den?" he asked, knowing the answer.

"Yes, let's do that," said Mr. Davis.

"Johnny can you go get your bath now? I want to talk to your Grammy." Valerie was anxious to get it over with.

"Okay, can I watch TV after I take my bath?"

"Yes, baby, you may, I'll be up later," she said. Going into Mrs. Davis' bedroom, they began to talk. "Sit down, please," said Valerie.

They sat at a small table along the wall.

"First of all, I want to apologize to you for lying to you. I was wrong to do that," she said.

"Next, I have to tell you that Mike and I have fallen in love, and we can't stand to be apart," she said, laying it on the line.

"Oh, my, is that so?" said Mrs. Davis.

"Yes, it is true. I know it happened fast. It wasn't planned; it just happened. But, we are both as sure as we can be, at this stage, that we really do feel we are deeply in love," she said.

"Well, this is quite a surprise; but, Valerie, if it is for real, then I am happy that you have found someone that really cares about you. Donald didn't treat you right; but that is neither here nor there. You are divorcing him, and no one knows where he is. I can't honestly say that I blame you; a young healthy beautiful woman like yourself is not going to wait forever hoping her husband is going to do right," she said.

"If Donald came back and became a saint, it wouldn't matter now," Valerie said, "I should have divorced him a long time ago. For over two years our marriage has been over and, whether Mike had come along or not, I had made up my mind that I was going to divorce Donald."

Shaking her head, Mrs. Davis said, "Yes, I know it hasn't been a marriage in a long time, Valerie, and it is too bad he got mixed up in that crowd."

They continued to talk, as did Mike and Mr. Davis in the den.

"Mike, what did the detective say today?"

"Well sir, they saw Donald and another guy, Larry Plott, in Vegas on Tuesday of last week and haven't seen them since."

"Neither one since then, huh?" asked Mr. Davis. "They saw Plott the next day, but haven't seen either one since then," he told him.

"I guess there wasn't anything else to report, was there?" Mr. Davis asked.

"No sir, unfortunately, there wasn't." Mike had decided not to tell him about the contract on his son's head. The man had been through enough although he was realistic about the situation and knew that Donald was in big trouble.

"Well thanks, Mike, for the information, all we can do is hope and pray for the best," he said.

"Yes sir, that is about all we can do. I am sorry that you have to go through this; I know it is a tough situation for you."

"Yes, he is my son, and I am sorry that he has taken the road that he has, but I cannot give him any more money to throw away. If the police catch him dealing drugs, they will put him in jail," he said.

Little did Mr. Davis know, Donald's worries were more than just being caught by the police. Mike didn't reveal anything more.

Valerie and Mrs. Davis were finishing up their talk.

"I am glad we talked and got everything out in the open between us," Valerie said.

"I am glad, also, honey, and I support you in your decision. You know that I love Mike; he is such a fine man. Carl was just saying yesterday what a good man he was, to be so young," Mrs. Davis said.

"Yes, and I love him so much; he makes me very happy," she said.

"Well, we will all work things out together, and don't worry about Carl. I am sure that he will be glad for you when he finds out. I'll take care of that, or we will, at an appropriate time."

"Thank you so very much for understanding," Valerie said, "I knew you would." They hugged and left the room.

"Well, Mike, how about a nightcap? We've done all we can do tonight."

"Yes, sir, that would be nice," said Mike.

Mr. Davis opened the den door and looked out just as the ladies had exited the bedroom.

"Ladies, would you care to join Mike and me in the den for a nightcap?" he asked.

"Why thank you, kind sir, we certainly would," said Mrs. Davis, speaking for both of them as Valerie smiled. She was relieved that it was in the open, at least with her mom, and she also could use that drink. They strolled into the den as Mr. Davis fixed the brandy.

He gave everyone a glass of brandy.

He then raised his glass as they stood watching him. "Here is to us," he said simply.

They all took a sip, and afterwards, Mrs. Davis went over and hugged Mike, kissing him on the cheek. Over her shoulder, Mike saw Valerie wink at him, but Mr. Davis did not.

"Mike, that is just my way of saying how happy I am that you are here, and how much you have meant to our family since you came here," she said.

"Why thank you; you folks have been very kind to me. It has worked out good here on the farm, I am very grateful for you and the job here," Mike said.

"Mike, of course I second what Jean just said. You have really helped take the strain off of me around here," said Mr. Davis.

They finished their drink as they chatted in the den. A little while later they left the den, and Mr. and Mrs. Davis announced they were going to bed.

They bid each other goodnight.

"Goodnight, you two. Mike and I are going for a short walk before we go to bed, so sleep tight," Valerie said.

"That's nice, it is a good night for it, so pleasant out this evening," Mrs. Davis said, as she walked to her bedroom.

Mike and Valerie walked out back.

"I forgot to ask if they saw any aliens today," Mike said, as they walked out the back gate.

Valerie smiled up at him.

"Let's go look at the field," she said.

They walked to the little hill and looked down to the cornfield. It had been all cut down, with just the short stubs remaining.

"Our beautiful cornfield is gone, Mike," she pouted, while feigning disappointment.

"Don't worry, it will grow back in time," he said, going along with her.

He reached for her, finding her eagerly waiting to find his lips as they embraced.

"How did your talk go?" he asked.

"Just great, Mike. Mom loves you and was happy for us. She realizes that my marriage has been over for a long time, and she is pulling for us," she said enthusiastically.

"It is nice to have her in our corner," he said.

"Yes it is, and I am sure my father-in-law will be, too, once he is aware of everything," she said.

"I hope you are right. It probably won't be long until he finds out about us," he surmised, since Mrs. Davis knew about them.

"I don't know; but you're probably right. He will suspect something, or she will tell him. I don't mind if she does; I want it to be out in the open," she said.

"Yes, it would be better in a way really, then we wouldn't have to be quite so careful around them. They would know that we loved each other, and we wouldn't have to stifle our love so much in the house."

"I know, baby, it will work out with them," she said.

They walked back to the house and went upstairs to go to bed. After tucking Johnny in bed, Valerie slipped over to Mike's room and got in his bed. When he came out of the bathroom, he discovered her in his bed, and had not heard her come in.

"This is a nice surprise in my bed," he said.

"Oh, darling," she said, and they began with a kiss, progressing rapidly to the place where they were enthusiastically sharing their passions.

Later on, before they went to sleep, they chatted some about their day.

"Mike, thanks for a nice day; I really enjoyed it and especially being with you. I enjoyed meeting, Jack, too; he is funny," she said.

"Yes, he is quite a guy. It was great being with you darling; I love you," he said.

Declaring her love for him, she snuggled closer and fell asleep.

For the next three weeks, the farm ran smoothly, and the crops were getting to market on time, with the profits increasing, now that Mike had things more organized and running well. They had not heard any more from Donald, but Mike had called the detective, and they had seen Larry Plott again in Vegas, but he had evaded the police.

Mike and Valerie were talking one night outside on the bench.

"Mike, I missed my period this month," she said emphatically.

"Oh, does that mean, ah, are you... or what does, ah, I mean, ah," Mike stammered, and they both laughed.

"I don't know for sure, I am going to the doctor tomorrow; but I think so, because I have gained a little weight and have been nauseous some in the morning a couple oftimes," she said.

"Do you think I am going to be a daddy?"

"Maybe so; how would you feel about that?" she said, anxious for his answer.

"I would love it. Just think, our own baby together! Oh, yes, that would be great!" He was excited, and she was glad.

"I hope I am, Mike. I would love to have your baby and give Johnny a brother or sister. I am going in the morning to the doctor, and we'll find out for sure," she said.

"Mike, I am so happy and excited about it; I hope I am pregnant," she said.

They kissed and went into the house.

The next morning when Valerie got back from the doctor, Mike was in the field. Valerie got on the golf cart and rode down to the field to see him.

"Mike!" she called, when she had spotted him in the field.

He heard her and came running over to her. "What did the doctor say?" he asked expectantly.

"It's true, Mike, I am!" she said, with a big smile on her face.

They embraced and smiled happily at each other. It was almost time for lunch, so they went to the house.

"Oh, Valerie, I am a happy man; you are going to have our baby!" He was, indeed, a happy man.

"What about Mr. Davis?" Mike asked with a worried look.

"My mom told him about us last night, and she told him that I was going to the doctor today," she said.

"They went into town early this morning and might be home now. They told me they would try to be back in time for lunch," she said.

"Good, we'll all have to talk, I guess," Mike said, looking a little nervous.

"It will be all right, darling," she said, reassuring him as she reached over and patted his hand.

"Yes, it will just have to be. You are going to have my baby; I can't believe I am going to be a father!" Mike was very happy.

When they reached the house, they both went in with big smiles. The Davises were there in the hallway and could read their minds, which was evidenced by the increasing smile on their faces, as they looked at them.

"You don't have to say a word; we can see it written all over your faces," Mr. Davis said, extending his opened arms toward Valerie.

She soon filled the arms of her father-in-law, and

Mrs. Davis filled Mike's arms, giving each other big hugs. Then Mike and Mr. Davis shook hands, and Mrs. Davis and Valerie hugged.

While the celebrating and congratulations were going around the room, Mr. Davis crooked his arm at them.

"Let's eat," he said, and each took their place in the dining room. They were all ecstatically happy about Valerie's condition. They seemed unconcerned that she was married to someone else, and the fact that they were not married. They all had faith that it was right and began to eat.

"Mike, Jean told me everything last night, and I was, and am, happy for you both. I was once young myself, and I am very pleased that you will one day be a part of our family in a real way, and not just as an employee. Plus the fact that there soon will be another baby runnmg through the house," Mr. Davis said.

Mike was glad that everyone was happy and accepting of the situation.

"Yes, that will take some getting used to, but I am very happy about it; and I do love Valerie very much, sir," he said, squeezing her hand under the table, and reaching over to give her a little kiss.

Mike and Valerie were greatly relieved that they could be more open, now that the air was cleared; their secret was out, and had been so well received.

They had a pleasant meal together, after which Mike went back to the fields to work, smiling happily.

Valerie and Mike looked forward to the day when the epoch they had experienced could be culminated in marriage. Things couldn't be better at the moment.

Little did he know, but was about to discover, just how quickly things could change.

CHAPTER

16

One week later on Monday morning, just as the family was finishing breakfast, Sally answered the doorbell. It was Detective Hawkins. She let him in and escorted him into the den.

"Mr. Davis, there is a Mr. Hawkins in the den to see you, sir," she said, when she had returned to the dining room.

Everyone stood and looked to the den as if they were staring at a rattlesnake, which was about to strike. Valerie moved over, and Mike put his arm around her. Mrs. Davis stood with eyes wide.

"I'll be right there, Sally, thank you," said Mr. Davis, as he put down his napkin and left the room.

Mr. Davis entered the den and closed the door. "Mr. Davis, I am Detective Lewis Hawkins," the detective said, as they shook hands. "Yes, sir, what is it?"

"Sir, you better sit down; I have some bad news," the detective said.

Mr. Davis sat down on a chair, and his eyes got wide. "Is it Donald?" he asked anticipatorily.

"Yes sir, we have found your son, sir. It is my unpleasant duty to inform you that he has been murdered. We found him in the

137

desert, where he had been buried in a shallow grave. Apparently, he was assassinated. I am sorry, sir; I know it is a shock to you," the detective said.

Mr. Davis was shocked, indeed, and held his hands together, rubbing them vigorously.

"Oh, my, I was afraid of something like this. Where is the body now?" he asked.

"It was brought to the Los Angeles Morgue, and an autopsy is being performed now. The forensic people are preparing their report. Is there a particular funeral home where we can take the body when we are finished?" he asked.

"Yes, Morgan's Funeral Home, if you would. We will be in touch with them; take clothes, make the necessary arrangements, and so forth," he said.

"Yes sir, we'll see that the body is taken there," he said.

"I must tell everyone," he stood up.

"Would you mind staying a minute, Detective Hawkins?" he asked.

"I'd be happy to, sir," he said, being very respectful throughout the difficult task of informing Mr. Davis of the tragic news about his son.

Mr. Davis opened the door and asked them to come in.

After they had all entered, except Johnny, who was outside, he closed the door.

"Mr. Hawkins just told me that they have located Donald, and he is dead," he told them.

"Oh, no! Where is Johnny?" Valerie cried.

"He is outside, honey," Mike said, "I will go get him and bring him to you here."

"Thank you, Mike," she said, as her mother-in-law hugged her. In a few minutes, Mike returned with Johrmy in tow by his hand. He took him to his mother, who told him that his father had died. Johrmy didn't seem to fully understand since he had never had an experience with death in the family before. They all tried to console each other, and the detective left after a while. It was a sad situation and, although they didn't expect a very pleasant outcome for Donald, they had not expected him to be murdered. That is something they hadn't considered although they knew, in the back of their minds, that it could happen; they just would not let themselves talk about such a thing. It had been as if something kept them from voicing the words, with the hope that, if they did not say those things, then they would not occur.

The ensuing days brought the completion of the autopsy and transfer of the body to the funeral home. Donald's funeral was the following Sunday.

It was then that the realization of Donald's death hit

Mrs. Davis and Johnny. The funeral was in the chapel of the funeral home, and both Mrs. Davis and Johnny broke down. Valerie shed some tears as well, but it really hit Mrs. Davis at that time. Her only son had been murdered, and a flood of good memories of him seemed to come back to her and overwhelm her. She remembered things that took place when he was a little boy, and then later on when things were better between Donald and Valerie. She and Valerie talked in a soft voice, before the funeral began, and consoled each other. Johnny was there also with his mother, and asked if his daddy would be back. Mike was very supportive, as was Mr. Davis. They took their places, and the funeral began. The pastor from their church performed the ceremony, and handled it very well, with great respect and dignity. They all assembled at the graveside, and Donald was laid to rest. Mrs. Davis especially showed much sorrow and pain at that time.

Ever the gentleman, Mr. Davis was right there to help her, as were Mike and Valerie.

They arrived back home, and Mrs. Davis went to her bedroom to lie down for a while. Valerie went with her, continuing to talk for a while and rest from the ordeal. It seemed to help them both to talk to each other about it. After all, no one had more intimate knowledge of Donald than they did.

Donald was a case of a man being caught up in the world of drugs and loan sharks. He made some bad decisions in the beginning and, with one thing leading to another thing, Donald was soon in over his head. By borrowing money to cover debts from his gambling, he only got deeper in debt, and it had to surface at some point. The more money he lost, the more he had to borrow to cover debts. Then he was borrowing from Peter to pay Paul, and started dealing in drugs to make some quick money to pay the debts. When the flow of the drugs was interrupted, then he had no way to pay, so the thugs killed him for nonpayment.

His spiral downward had taken over two years, and Johnny and Valerie had suffered through it on the ranch. Valerie cared for Donald in the beginning, but he rapidly descended until there was not any marriage left to save. Then she resented the way she was being treated, and finally filed for divorce.

It was shortly after she had filed that she and Mike fell in love. They were very happy and couldn't wait to be married, and not have to sneak around anymore. They were very excited about having a baby together.

The next few days brought Valerie and Mrs. Davis together more as they grieved Donald's death, and gradually began to find a measure of peace concerning the situation. Complete healing would take a long time if it ever occurred. Each of them had come to a point of acceptance, however, and could slowly begin to function again in the family.

There were still occasional outbursts of crying when Mrs. Davis would recall something or be thinking about Donald, but slowly she began to heal and integrate back into the family.

Mr. Davis and Mike were very supportive and helpful to Valerie and Mrs. Davis. Mr. Davis was a strong man and had his own grief to deal with as he supported his wife and Valerie. His acceptance of the facts seemed to be more matter-of-fact, and he understood the results of bad decisions. It was not that he didn't care; he cared very much for Donald, his only son, and he had done everything he possibly could have done for him. Donald's death hurt Mr. Davis very much, but he seemed to accept it sooner than Mrs. Davis did. It was a tragedy that would hurt them all for a long time, and one that would cause pain, especially for Mrs. Davis, for the rest of their lives.

A week after the funeral, Mike and Valerie were walking in the backyard one night. Mike turned to Valerie and looked her into the eyes.

"Valerie, I love you, and want you to be my wife; will you marry me?"

"Oh, Mike! Yes, I will! I would love to be your wife."

They went back to the house and told Mr. and Mrs. Davis and Johnny about their plans to get married. They were happy for them and heartily congratulated them.

Mike called his folks in West Virginia and told them the news.

The following weekend they were all assembled in Las Vegas for the wedding. After the ceremony, the Davises returned home. Mike and Valerie spent the next two nights in Vegas for a mini-honeymoon, before returning to the ranch, promising each other a real honeymoon later on. They felt relieved that they could now proclaim their love to the whole world and could live together as man and wife.

As Valerie grew in her pregnancy, everyone was becoming excited about the prospects of having a baby in the house. Mike had moved over to Valerie's bedroom with her. Mrs. Davis and Valerie had already started decorating the room Mike had vacated, which would become the new baby's room.

Although adjusting to Donald's death was somewhat unnerving at first, it did bring with it an abrupt finality and solution to the stalemate that Valerie was in. Donald's death had left Valerie free to marry Mike without waiting for the divorce to be finalized.

The marriage had brought them closer, if that was possible, and their relationship grew even stronger. Mike had not only gained a wife and family, but he had gained a son, and Johnny was happy to have Mike as his step father.

Everything was going well, and they were very happy together. The fields were producing very well, and the business was growing under Mike's direction.

It was late August now, and it had been exceptionally hot the last two weeks. The sultry weather was present throughout the valley. The humidity hung suspended over them like a canopy just as the grapes hung over the arbors. The vapors of steam formed ghostly figures, which gave a brief appearance, and then quickly rose to join the clouds forming overhead. The morning's sunshine burned away the dew that covered the sweltering earth.

Monday morning, the thirtieth of August, found Mike in the field, picking cantaloupes and placing them on the truck nearby. A large field of cantaloupes would be harvested that week and sent to market.

Mr. and Mrs. Davis, along with Johnny, had gone to San Bernardino that morning to see a business associate and buyer. Mrs. Davis and Johnny would have time to do a little shopping while Mr. Davis attended his meeting.

It was early afternoon, and Mike had returned to the field after having his lunch. He continued to work until that evening when Valerie rode the golf cart down to the field to find him.

"Mike, come here quickly!" she shouted, as she spotted him in the field.

Mike rushed over to where she had stopped at the edge of the field.

"What is it Valerie, what is wrong?" He could see she was distressed.

"Mr. Davis just called, and he can't find Mrs. Davis and Johnny," she explained.

"They were to meet for lunch, and they didn't show up at the restaurant. He has looked everywhere and has notified the police that they are missing. I am getting worried about them."

Mike slid into the golf cart beside her, and they went to the house.

Arriving at the house, Sally advised them that Mr. Davis had called and was on the way home.

They anxiously waited for his arrival home and, in a few minutes, he came through the door.

"Mike, Valerie, they are gone! I looked everywhere and could not find them," Mr. Davis said, out of breath from hurrying in to share the grim news.

"What do you think has happened to them?" Valerie was very upset and nervous.

"I don't know. I was supposed to meet them for lunch, and they didn't show up. Then I went to several different stores, where Jean shops from time to time, and I could not find them. Finally I went to the police, and they are searching now." Mr. Davis was nervous and upset.

Sally was there and had been listening.

"Mr. Davis, may I fix you something to eat, sir?" Sally asked, realizing that he had not eaten his lunch.

"No thank you, Sally, I am going to fix a drink." He went to the den and began to fix a drink.

"We'll join you for one," said Valerie, as they followed him into the den.

They had their drinks and, in a few minutes, Sally came in with a plate full of sandwiches, determined that they all should eat something. They all did eat some of the sandwiches.

"Oh, Mike, what can we do; poor Johnny and his Grammy, where can they be?" Valerie was getting more upset.

Mike went over and put his arm around her, trying to comfort her.

"Maybe you had better go lie down for a while, darling; there is nothing we can do right now."

"Maybe I will go up for a little while and rest," Valerie said, as she walked toward the door. "Call me if you hear anything, darling."

"I will, and I'll be up in a little while to check on you," said Mike. "Mr. Davis and I will be here, and I am going to call the police in a while."

Sally escorted Valerie upstairs to her bed.

Mr. Davis and Mike waited in the den and had another drink. No calls came in for the next three hours, so Mr. Davis called the station and talked to the police. They were still out looking for them, and there was no news at all as to their whereabouts. There was nothing they could do but wait.

Sally made them some coffee and went home for the evening. Darkness slowly claimed its time and moved in. They waited until midnight, and then called the police again. Nothing new, was the report. Mike and Mr. Davis decided to call it a night and try to sleep, although they didn't think they could.

Eventually they did fall asleep, sometime in the middle of the night.

They woke up and got up early as usual, just as they automatically did, when they were working. They let Valerie sleep in while they had breakfast.

After breakfast, while they were having coffee, the phone rang. Mr. Davis answered the phone.

"Hello?"

"You did? That's good; and nothing on Jean, you say?"

"Okay, then, that's fine. We'll see you soon, and thanks."

Mr. Davis hung up the phone and gave his report. "Well, they have found Johnny. Apparently, a cab driver found him wandering around on the street last night. They haven't found Jean yet."

"They are on the way over here with Johnny now," he added.

Mike went upstairs and woke Valerie and told her the news. She was ecstatic; yet her joy was stifled since Mrs. Davis had not yet been found. She got up and shortly joined everyone downstairs.

The policeman soon brought Johnny home. He was embraced by his mother and looked-over, carefully. Johnny looked tired, and his clothes were dirty, and a tear was in a leg of his pants. His arms had abrasions, on which the police had put bandages.

They gave Johnny some food, and he ate a small amount while he told his story.

"Grammy and I came out of Jones department store, and this man grabbed me and threw me in the back seat of this car. Then he grabbed Grammy and put her in the front seat. He took off driving down the street. I thought I should get out of there because I thought he might hurt us. When he slowed down at a stoplight, I opened the car door and ran out of the car. My pants caught on something, and I tore them. The car was still moving, but not too fast, when I jumped out. I rolled over on the road and hurt my arms. I didn't cry though, Mommy, I didn't even cry."

"Oh, Johnny, you were a big boy, and I am glad you were not hurt worse than the abrasions on your arms," Valerie said.

Johnny took another spoonful of soup and continued to tell his story.

"Now that mean old man has Grammy, and I wish he didn't, Mommy. He won't hurt Grammy, will he?" Johnny said, as his eyes started to water.

"I hope not, honey; we will try to find her. You eat your dinner and then I am going to take you up for a nice bath and get you all cleaned up. Where did you go after you got out of the car?"

"I just walked around the street, and I got lost, and there was nobody around and, when it got dark, I hid behind this big trash can in an alley. I stayed there and fell asleep on some cardboard that I had found. I woke up when I heard a cat crying, and I ran out of the alley and walked down the street a while. Then this man in the cab came along and stopped and picked me up, and took me to the police. He was a nice man, Mommy, not like that mean old man that took Grammy."

"Yes, darling, he was a very nice man." Valerie put her hand on Johnny's arm and patted him.

Valerie then took Johnny upstairs for a bath.

The police didn't have much to go on in their search. Johnny had told them that the car was black in color and a four-door. Other than that, there was no other description of the car.

Johnny told them the man was medium built, and had short dark hair. That was all they had concerning the perpetrator. Not much at all to go on, to find the man who now held Mrs. Davis.

The members of the household were very thankful for the fact that Johnny had been returned to them. Mr. Davis insisted on giving the cab driver a monetary reward, and asked for his name and address. The policeman promised to supply it when he returned to the station.

Fear and unrest was still with them, as Mrs. Davis was still missing. Valerie had put Johnny down for a nap after his bath. When she returned downstairs, she joined Mike and Mr. Davis in the den. She went over and put her arms around Mr. Davis, who responded in kind.

"Oh, I am so sorry," said Valerie, "I know you are worried. We all are."

"Yes, Valerie, I am very concerned and feel very helpless. There is nothing we can do but wait for the police to find her, or to hear something."

After she felt she had comforted Mr. Davis all she could, she moved over by Mike, who put his arm around her. She didn't want to be separated from him or leave his side at all now.

When Mike decided to go to the fields for a while and help out, Valerie went with him. Mr. Davis encouraged them to go and to occupy their minds, saying that he would remain in the house, close to the phone, and he and Sally would look after Johnny as well.

The physical activity relieved their anxiety some, although Valerie didn't try to do too much. She just wanted to be near Mike at that time and worked a little to occupy her mind. It seemed to help them both, and they worked a couple of hours. Then they returned to the house as the workers finished the job, and headed off to market.

Sally had made some lemonade, which they enjoyed with Mr. Davis in the den.

"The policeman called and gave me the name and address of the cab driver. I have a card a and check ready to go out in the mail tomorrow,"

"That's good, Dad, and very generous ofyou," Valerie acknowledged.

"Well, it seemed the least I could do for him, getting little Johnny to the police and looking after him."

"Yes, I am very grateful to that man," Valerie said, "I don't know what I would have done if something had happened to Johnny."

They soon went into the dining room and had their meal together. Johnny joined them, looking much better after his nap. After their meal, they all went for a short walk together. Sally, offering to listen for the phone, stayed behind to do the dishes and other chores before she went home for the night. Sally and her husband, Jim, had been good and faithful employees for a long time, and had become a part of the family. Jim maintained the aesthetics of the gardens and lawn, keeping the place immaculate and so alive with an infinite variety of flowers, offering vibrant colors very pleasing to all who saw them.

As they leisurely strolled along, watching the setting sun slowly being drawn over the horizon, it appeared as if it was a shade being pulled down. The vast array of oranges and reds filled the sky before them, ever changing in their hues and intensity. The captivating beauty of the sunset gave them momentary relief for their minds and an escape from their troubles, even if it were only for a few minutes.

Fields of lush green vegetables were a sight to behold, along with the grapes hanging in full bunches on the arbors, in the distance. Their color beginning to turn from green to purple as they approached harvest, and the making of the wine.

Standing mesmerized, their eyes drunk in the beauty before them, while inhaling the aroma of the exhilarating fresh air.

With darkness beginning to fall, they returned to the house for the evening. After having a nightcap together, Sally went home, and they all turned in for the evening.

Valerie stayed with Johnny until he went to sleep; then she moved to Mike's room and slid into bed beside of him.

As their lips came together, they embraced lovingly, while their passion soon increased in intensity to the point of ecstasy and release, declaring their love for each other.

When they returned to earth, and their heart rate and pulse descended to normal, they drifted off together into a deep sleep. By wrapping their arms around each other, it seemed they could find solace, and separate themselves from their troubles, if only for a while.

CHAPTER

17

The phone seemed louder in the middle of the night, suddenly awakening Valerie and Mike. Little Johnny had slept through it, but Mr. Davis heard it and answered. "Hello?"

"I have your wife, and I want twenty-thousand dollars. I will call you back later with more details."

That was the extent of the phone conversation. With chills running up his spine, he went to the den for a drink. Shortly, Valerie and Mike joined him. It was 4:00A.M.

They waited and consoled each other until 6:00 A.M.

Then Mr. Davis called Detective Lewis Hawkins and told him what had happened. Detective Hawkins said he would be out to see them that morning.

The detective arrived about 8:00 A.M. Sally had gotten there earlier, and they had finished eating breakfast; however, Detective Hawkins joined them for coffee in the den.

"I brought this recording device that I want to hook to your phone," the detective said. "All incoming calls will be recorded and, we will try to trace the calls. Please call me immediately when they call back, no matter what time it is, whether it is day or night."

"Yes, I will call you, as you say. In the meantime, I am going to the bank and get twenty-thousand dollars, like he said."

"Well, I can't advise you there; sometimes these people will do what they say in a kidnapping, and sometimes... well what I mean is that paying the ransom will not guarantee your wife's safety. That will have to be your decision about the money," Detective Hawkins continued. "There isn't much we can do or plan until he calls back with his demands. Once he does call, then we will set up a plan of action." This experienced detective had been through this sort of thing many times in the past.

He connected the recording device to the phone and left the house to return to his duties.

Mr. Davis went to his bank in town and withdrew twenty thousand dollars from his account, preparing to pay the money, without the blink of an eye, if there was even a slight chance that his wife would be returned.

Upon his return from the bank, Valerie and Mike reported to Mr. Davis there had been no phone calls while he was away. Then, for a change of pace, and to get out a little while, Mike, Valerie and Johnny went to the field to work until time for their evening meal.

After dinner at 7:00P.M., while assembled for coffee in the den, the phone rang, causing everybody to jump. Mr. Davis quickly activated the recorder, and then picked up the phone.

"Hello?" he said, expectantly.

"Did you get the money yet?"

"Yes, I have the money."

"Good, now listen carefully. You must follow my instructions exactly, and I will return your wife to you if you do. Any police involvement, whatsoever, and the deal will be off."

"Can I speak to her, just to know that she is all right and that you have her?" Mr. Davis asked.

"Hold on a minute."

It was quiet for a minute, which seemed like an hour as the tension built.

"Hello, Carl, are you there?"

"Jean, is that you, are you all right, honey?"

"Yes, I am all right dear; he has not hurt me, but please do as he says.

"I will, and don't worry; we have Johnny here, at home, with us."

"Okay, that is enough, are you satisfied now?" " "Yes, that was her; please don't hurt her."

"Put the money in a brown paper bag and go to Wingfoot and Avalon Boulevard in LA tomorrow night at 7:00P.M, exactly, and listen for the phone at the booth there, and I will instruct you then, " with that, the phone went dead.

Mr. Davis called Detective Hawkins immediately and told him of the conversation.

"Okay, Mr. Davis, we are formulating our plan of action, but it will be done in such a way, and at a distance, so as not to jeopardize your wife's safety," Detective Hawkins explained, "I will be there at your house in the morning to explain our plan to you. He probably won't call any more tonight."

"Yes sir, we'll look for you then in the morning. If he does call back, I will notify you immediately, although he did say not to involve the police."

"Yes, you call me if you get any more calls. I'll see you in the morning."

It would be another long night of worry and stress. Mike and Mr. Davis were looking over a city map of Los Angeles while Valerie put Johnny to bed.

Having found the intersection where they were to go,

Mike thought it would be a good idea for him to go early and watch, from a distance, what took place, just in case he was needed. They would talk to Detective Hawkins in the morning. At midnight, just before they turned in for the night, the phone rang again.

"Hello?"

"You all set to do as I said?"

"Yes, I will be there at 7:00P.M. at the phone booth.

"Don't fail to be, or else!"

"I'll be there," Mr. Davis said, but then realized he was talking to a dead phone. The man had hung up.

He immediately called the detective, telling him of the phone call, and then they all bid each other goodnight. After that, he went to bed. There was not anything else they could do tonight. Mr. Davis thought they all should try to get some sleep while they could, because they didn't know when the man would call back again. They had received their instructions, and Mr. Davis was prepared to carry them out.

The night proved to be a long one for all of them, as they had trouble falling asleep under the tension and stress of the prospects of the coming events. Eventually, however, they did sleep sporadically.

At six o'clock the next morning, they were all up and heard Jose knocking on the back door. Sally let him in, and he went to the dining room where everyone had just started to eat breakfast.

Mr. Davis saw him and pointed to a chair.

"Sit down Jose, and have breakfast with us."

"Well, thank you, sir. I will. I really came to tell you that all the workers and I are very sorry, sir, to hear about Mrs. Davis, and to tell you that our good thoughts are with her and the family. If we can help in any way, we will do whatever you say. Also, I wanted to tell you that the work is going well, and everybody is determined to get the crops to market on time," Jose said, beginning to eat the food that Sally had placed before him.

"Thank you, Jose, for your offer. There is nothing anybody can do right now, but I appreciate the offer and I will remember it, should something come up that you, or the others, can do to help. Also, I knew I could depend on you to get the crops in. The fields are producing better than ever now, and our business is growing. We might have to hire more workers, so if you know of some who would like to work here, let me know, and we will talk to them. Either Mike or myself will talk to them."

"Yes sir, I will be on the lookout for some workers,"

Jose said, as he took another mouthful of eggs and washing it down with coffee.

After they finished breakfast, Jose returned to the fields to work while the others went to the den and waited for the detective to arrive.

It was not long until Detective Hawkins arrived, and Sally showed him into the den.

"Mr. Davis, we have contacted the phone company, and they will be in on this surveillance with us all the way," he began.

"When the phone rings here, they will begin to trace the call. If you can hold him on the phone by asking a pertinent question, then do so; but try not to be too obvious when doing this. The reason is that you might alert him to what you are doing. We will be in unmarked vehicles, watching the phone booth from a distance, and we will hear your conversation with him. Whatever instructions he gives you, we will hear them. Just remain as calm as you can, and comply with his instructions."

"Yes sir, I will do that all right, I want to get her back to us safely and in one piece."

"Mike, I have instructed the dispatcher to put you and Mr. Davis through to me whenever you call my office. Call me if you feel the need, and they will put you through to me. I am in the process of procuring a hand held police radio for you, and I will send it to you as soon as the paperwork goes through for it. Then we can have two-way communications, and it won't be necessary for you to phone the office since we'll be able to talk direct, using the two-way radio. Mr. Davis will need to use the phone to call the office, as I don't want to take a chance on the villain finding a police radio in his car or on him," the detective said. He had thought of everything, it seemed.

"Yes sir, that will be great to have and whatever I can do to help, I will do it," Mike said, conveniently omitting the fact that he planned to be watching the phone booth as well.

"Well, that's about it; just do what the man says and we'll be watching, basically, that is it," the detective said, standing to leave.

"Thanks for your help, I appreciate it," Mr. Davis said, extending his hand to him. They shook hands, and then Detective Hawkins left the house.

About 2:00 P.M. an unmarked police car pulled up, and a young policeman delivered the police radio and instructed Mike on its operation. Mike tried it out.

"Mike calling Mr. Hawkins. Come in."

"This is Mr. Hawkins; I see you got the radio, Mike, over?"

"Yes sir, I hear you good, over."

"Ten-Four, Mike. Call when you need to, out."

The young policeman left, and Mike prepared to go into the city ahead of time to find a nearby place where he could watch the phone booth. Mr. Davis would leave at 5:30P.M. That should get him there, thirty minutes early, to wait for the call. At 4:00 P.M. Mike kissed Valerie goodbye, and headed into the city with his radio on the seat beside of him.

When Mike arrived at the intersection that had been designated, he drove one block past the phone booth, at South Main Street and Wingfoot. He went into a service station and parked where he could look straight ahead, through the windshield, and see the phone booth. He had a pair of binoculars with him, and had approximately one hour and fifteen minutes to wait until 7:00P.M. He walked into the service station and got a coke and returned and took up his vigilance. He had a clear view of the phone booth.

Mike saw some cars going by slowly, and wondered if any of them were police cars.

About 6:30P.M., Mike saw Mr. Davis pull up and park by the curb near the phone booth. They continued to wait.

At 7:00P.M. the phone rang, and Mr. Davis got out of the car and answered it. "Hello?"

"Oakwood and South Western Avenue. Yes, I know where it is, and I am going right now."

Mr. Davis got back in the car and drove off. Mike radioed Detective Hawkins.

"Detective Hawkins, this is Mike, come in."

"This is Lewis Hawkins, what's up, Mike?"

"I was just wondering where he is going."

"Oakwood and South Western Avenue, Mike; another phone booth. The guy is going to run him around some now. You be careful out there ifyou are tailing him."

"Yes sir, I will, out"

Mike got out his map and found the address and went back four blocks, and took a right onto South Western. He drove down several blocks until he came to Oakwood. He went one block past Oakwood, and turned around, and parked along the curb. He saw Mr. Davis sitting in his car, which was parked down the street by the phone booth.

In a few minutes the phone apparently rang, as Mr.

Davis answered it. "Hello?"

"Listen carefully; I'll only say this one time. Go to Redlands; it will take you about an hour and a half to get there. Go down Fifth Avenue until you come to Crafton. On the corner is a house with four columns on the front porch. The porch extends across the entire front of the house. The front porch light will be on.

Five Hundred Crafton is the house number of the street address and is under the light. When we see you parked in front of the house, we will send your wife out to the front porch. When you see her, take the bag of money and place it by her on the porch, and take her and go immediately. Any cops or anyone shows up, and you both get it. Do you understand the instructions?"

"Yes, I understand, and I am on the way. I should be there about 9:30P.M., depending on traffic.

"Okay, get started; we are waiting for you."

Mike watched and called Detective Hawkins, giving him the information, while he looked on his map to find Redlands, and set out to go there. Mike, following Mr. Davis at a distance, didn't know if he would lose him or not since the traffic was very heavy.

Managing to keep Mr. Davis in view, they pulled into Redlands in about an hour and forty-five minutes. Mike slacked off now, and didn't want to be seen. Pulling in by the curb, some two blocks away from the house, he watched and waited. Mr. Davis waited for his wife to appear on the porch. Mike pulled up closer, and parked the car along the curb about a half block away.

It was a dark as Mike watched a lady come out onto the porch. Just then Mr. Davis walked to the porch and set down the bag containing the money. He and Mrs. Davis returned to the car, and drove off immediately. Just as they drove off, a short man dressed in dark clothes, opened Mike's passenger door and got in. He was holding a gun, pointed toward Mike.

"Well, well, what have we here?"

Mike didn't say anything. This man had completely surprised him. him.

"Pull down there in front of the house," the man told

Mike did as he said, and parked in front of the house. "Now, slide across the seat and get out and go in the house," the man told him, as he opened the car door and got out.

Mike complied with his commands. They went in the front door. On the way into the house, the man picked up the bag of money. Until they entered, the house was empty. *The man must have instructed Mrs. Davis what to do, and probably threatened her,* " Mike surmised.

When they got inside, Mike received further instructions.

"Okay, right out the back door and into the alley."

They got into a car that was parked in the alley, and Mike drove as the man held the gun on him, giving directions as to where to turn.

The police radio had been left in his car, and he wondered where the police were. If they were around, the man had given them the slip by going through the house the way he did. They went to Interstate 15, and drove to Barstow and, following instructions, Mike pulled through a drive-thru restaurant and ordered burgers and drinks.

Pulling out of there, they drove to a secluded house on the outskirts of town. They had gone about an eighth of a mile down a graveled road to reach the house. Mike pulled into the garage and got out of the car as directed.

"Okay, inside," the man   said, following Mike through the kitchen door.

"Now, get downstairs," the man directed.

"I have to make a move; if he gets me in the basement, there's no telling what he will do. I need to make a move now, " Mike thought.

Just as Mike started downstairs, he turned very fast and knocked the gun free from the man's hand. The gun fell down the steps and landed about halfway down on a step. The man looked surprised, and turned and ran out the door, and across the field, with the bag of money in his hand. Mike took off running after him. He had no fear, now that the gun was gone, and he was gaining on the man.

"You might as well surrender!" Mike called to him.

The man kept running and ran into an industrial complex, whichjoined the field.

American Steel Company had a complex there of several buildings, and the man ran inside one of them. He had run into the prefabrication shop of the company, where they cut and bent the reinforcing bars that supported concrete. The concrete reinforcing bars were in all shapes and sizes; each one, which had been shaped, was stacked in its own pile.

The man ran up the long steel steps to the upper level, which had grating for a floor. Mike pursued him up the steps. There was no one there at that hour. It was very hot in there, and got hotter the further they climbed. Only a portion of the plant lights had been left on, leaving it dark in some places.

When the man had reached the second level, and ran to the end of the grating, there was no place left to go. There was a steel beam, which led to another grating, and if the man could reach that grating, then there were steps down to the ground level. The beam was only about six inches wide, and suspended out in the open some fifteen feet from the wall. And, it was open all the way to the end of the building on the other side of it. *"Surely the man won't try to walk across that, for the twenty:feet or so, in this poorly-lit place, "* thought Mike.

Just then the man straddled the guardrail and climbed over it and onto the steel beam.

"Don't try it, man!" called Mike, as he watched in disbelief. The beam was about thirty-feet off the ground, and was right above a pile of the reinforcing bars that had been bent in an L-shape, and stacked there with the short end of the "L" looking up.

Paying no attention to Mike's warning, the man proceeded to inch his way across the steel beam. Mike stood and watched in disbelief with his hands on the handrail.

About half way across, his feet had become coated with the fine powdery steel dust that had accumulated there over time. It was about a half inch thick when he started across. His shoes were very slick now.

As the man had now reached the point of no return, standing in the middle of the beam, thirty-feet up without railings close to him, and nothing around to grab, he realized he hopelessly was stranded.

"Help! It is slick and the beam is sagging!"

"Keep walking, man; it is your only chance; keep going!"

Mike tried to encourage him, but there was nothing else he could do for the man. It would not do any good to even consider going out on the beam after him. There wasn't anything he could do but try to encourage him to continue on across and reach the other side.

"Just keep walking, man, and keep going," Mike told him.

The man still clung to the bag of money.

"My feet are slick, and my legs are shaking!"

"Keep walking man; it is your only chance!"

Just then the man tried to take another step and his foot slipped. He began falling, hitting his hip on the rail, which turned his body over, stomach down. He continued to fall, and landed below on the upturned reinforcing bar, which went right through his body. The reinforcing bar could be seen sticking all the way through him. It happened so fast, he had not screamed, but when he had landed on the bar, he groaned, dying instantly afterwards.

"Oh no, Oh no!" Mike said softly, in a whisper.

Mike's knees got weak, and he held the rail for a minute to gain his composure. He looked down and saw the man stuck on the bar, noticing the moneybag had fallen on the concrete, beside the pile of bars, and was still intact.

He slowly walked down the long staircase that he had climbed up, and retrieved the bag of money. Mike held the bag and looked at the man a minute, while he reached over and pulled his wallet out of his pants. He looked at the drivers' license. It read "Larry Plott."

Returning the wallet, he left the building and walked to the road and saw a service station in the distance and started walking toward it. When he got there, he called Detective Hawkins and told him what had happened. He said he would be right out. Mike also told him about his car, and that the radio was in it. The detective said he would have the car taken to Mr. Davis's ranch. Mike waited at the service station for the detective. He arrived in about thirty minutes.

"Hop in, Mike, and we'll ride down there to the scene," the detective called to Mike, driving along side of the phone booth, where Mike had remained while he waited.

"Mike, I am glad to see that you are all right. By the way, I have called an ambulance to come out here. They should be here shortly," he said, as Mike took the passenger's seat.

"Yes, I am fine; I assume Mrs. Davis is okay?"

"Yes, she is fine, and home now."

They drove through the opened gate of the plant. Mike directed Detective Hawkins inside and explained what had happened. They even walked upstairs, where he had chased Larry Plott, and Mike showed him where Plott had crossed over the handrail. He showed him where he was on the beam when he fell. Then they went downstairs just as the ambulance arrived.

Mike and Detective Hawkins finished up their tour, and the detective then instructed the men to place Larry Plott in the ambulance and to take him to the morgue. The coroner was there and, after finishing his job, everyone soon left the scene of the accident.

Detective Hawkins took Mike home and, after dropping him off at the front door and getting the radio, he told Mike he would go on home and would not go in this time. Mike's car was in the driveway and Mike walked over and got the radio and handed it to Detective Hawkins.

"Thanks, Detective Hawkins, for everything," Mike said, as he shook the detective's hand.

"You bet, Mike, and now go on in and see everyone, I know they are waiting for you," he said, driving away.

CHAPTER

18

Mike walked through the door and immediately his arms were filled, as Valerie greeted him with hugs and kisses. He handed Mr. Davis the bag of money, who was watching, with a smile on his face. He then hugged Mrs. Davis, who was visibly shaken by all the activity.

"Mike, thank you for coming for me and looking out for Carl," she said.

"Ah, that was nothing, just what anyone would do."

"How about a drink, Mike?" Mr. Davis asked.

"Yes, I would love one."

They went into the den and had a drink together.

Mike hugged Johnny goodnight, and Valerie took him up to his bed. She returned shortly, and Mike told them about what had happened to Larry Plott.

Mrs. Davis looked none the worse for wear, after her ordeal, and she said that Larry Plott didn't hurt her. She said he was just after the money so that he could pay his debt and, thus, not end up like Donald. Larry Plott planned to use part of the ransom money to make his escape. It was not to be.

After another drink, they all turned in for the night. Mike took a long shower, and then got into his bed where his loving wife was waiting for him.

They fully celebrated that everybody was back home safe, and later fell asleep in each other's arms.

Gradually, in the coming days and weeks, a normalcy began to return to the ranch as time started to heal the pain of Donald's death, and the stressful time that accompanied that period.

Valerie was showing for sure now, and they anticipated the arrival of their child with hope and joy.

The time came for the harvesting of the grapes and the making of the wine. The other crops had done very well that year, and it was declared the best year ever. No doubt Mike had a hand in accomplishing that feat.

The little house down in the corner of the property had been completely renovated now, and Jose and his family had decided to move into the house. It had turned out really well, and would make a nice place for them to live.

Several new acres had been plowed, and crops would be planted there as the farm expanded. There was an ever increasing demand for their vegetables and fruit, and the expansions were just the first of many that would be done in the coming year.

As time went on, the pain of the past seemed to dim, while the prospects for the future became brighter.

Mike and Valerie had talked about going back east to West Virginia, for a visit, after the baby was born, and was big enough to travel. Mike's mother was happy for them and excited to become a grandmother.

The great love that Mike and Valerie had seemed to rush into, had only become stronger with time. The more they were together, the more they were convinced that they had definitely made the right decision. Valerie was a good and faithful companion for Mike, and was absolutely crazy about him. Mike, conversely, was just as crazy about her, and couldn't stand to be away from her. They were not only great lovers, but also great friends.

With the coming of their first child, they were very happy on the farm.

The beauty surrounding them, of the rolling hills and farm, was breathtaking. The fields full of fruit and vegetables were full of color and beauty, as well as offering a delicious smelling aroma.

As things settled down and the tensions dissipated, the farm began to run like a well-oiled machine, with each part doing its job, and contributing to the welfare of all of them.

Even little Johnny could be seen, from time to time, laughing and working in the fields for the fun of it. The workers loved having him around. Sometimes his buddy, Carlos, would help and they would work together for a while. Then they would go off to play ball, or do something they wanted to do.

It was a great place for a child to grow up.

The leader of the drug ring had not been captured, but they had some leads, and Detective Hawkins told Mike they thought it was someone in the film industry. They were still following leads and pursuing the capture of the leaders of the ring.

One night after a long day of work, Mike and Valerie were lying in bed. In the distance, Mike detected the faint wail of a train's whistle. Mike smiled and looked at Valerie, who smiled back at him. She had also heard the whistle.

"I hear the whistle calling, darling."

"It can call all it wants to, but you can't go," she said, reading his thoughts, and gripping him tighter.

Just then, the phone rang. Mike picked it up.

"Hello?"

"Hello Mike, this is Reba."

The End

Now available through
bookstores everywhere

The Release of the Albatross
By
Ernest L. Anderson

Brad Thomas, a young man from West Virginia moved to Richmond, Virginia to attend medical school. Soon after his arrival there, he was arrested for a robbery he did not commit. He was convicted of the crime and sent to prison. This is the story of how he refuses to accept his imprisonment, and uses his wit to gain his freedom. He soon realizes that being out of prison is not really being free, if you are on the run. The only way he will ever really be free is to pursue the robber himself. He falls in love with a beautiful nurse, who along with his friend, help him to track down the real robber. His romance flourishes as the tension increases in their efforts to prove his innocence.

Now available through
bookstores everywhere

Whispers from the Hills
A mountaineer's journal
By
Ernest L. Anderson

Whispers from the Hills is a collection of three essays, thirty-nine poems, and three Haiku. The three essays vividly depict the life of a young boy growing up in Fairlea, West Virginia in late 1949, and the early 1950's.

The poems have something for everyone, from the very young, to the senior citizen. The Humorous section will have you rolling in the aisles as the author pokes fun at the ordinary things of life. The Contemplative section will make you think, and perhaps see things from a different perspective. The Love section will transport you into a realm to which everyone should go at sometime in life. Once there, you might never want to leave.

www.ingramcontent.com/pod-product-compliance
Lightning Source LLC
Chambersburg PA
CBHW021151190726
48288CB00008B/2922